Rescue at Boomerang Bend

Books by Robert Elmer

ADVENTURES DOWN UNDER

THE YOUNG UNDERGROUND

ROBERT ELMER

RESCUE AT BOOMERANG BEND

BETHANY HOUSE PUBLISHERS
MINNEAPOLIS, MINNESOTA 55438

Rescue at Boomerang Bend
Copyright © 1998
Robert Elmer

Cover illustration by Chris Ellison
Cover design by Peter Glöege

Unless otherwise identified, Scripture quotations are from the King James
Version of the Bible.

Published by Bethany House Publishers
A Ministry of Bethany Fellowship, Inc.
11300 Hampshire Avenue South
Minneapolis, Minnesota 55438

Printed in the United States of America.

Library of Congress Cataloging-in-Publication Data

Elmer, Robert.
    Rescue at Boomerang Bend / by Robert Elmer.
        p. cm.—(Adventures down under ; 3)
    Summary: In Australia in 1868, twelve-year-old Patrick continues to
search for his missing father, who has been convicted of a crime he did not
commit and has been forced into hiding out in the bush.
    ISBN 1–55661–925–1 (pbk.)
    [1. Robbers and outlaws—Fiction. 2. Australia—Fiction.] I. Title.
II. Series: Elmer, Robert. Adventures down under ; 3.
PZ7.E4794Re   1997
[Fic]—dc21   97–33856
                                                                   CIP
                                                                    AC

To Grandma Ayers,
our family's "pioneer."

MEET ROBERT ELMER

ROBERT ELMER is the author of THE YOUNG UNDERGROUND series, as well as many magazine and newspaper articles. He lives with his wife, Ronda, and their three children, Kai, Danica, and Stefan (and their dog, Freckles), in a Washington State farming community just a bike ride away from the Canadian border.

CONTENTS

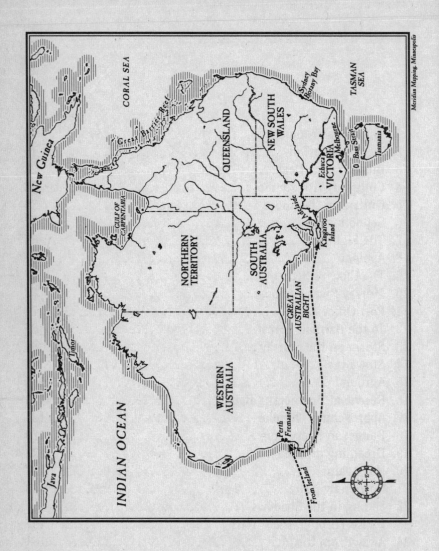

CORAL SEA

New Guinea

Great Barrier Reef

QUEENSLAND

NEW SOUTH WALES

Sydney
Botany Bay

TASMAN SEA

GULF OF CARPENTARIA

NORTHERN TERRITORY

SOUTH AUSTRALIA

Adelaide

Kangaroo Island

Echuca
VICTORIA
Melbourne

0 Bass Strait

Tasmania

Timor

WESTERN AUSTRALIA

GREAT AUSTRALIAN BIGHT

Perth
Fremantle

Java

INDIAN OCEAN

From Ireland

Meridian Mapping, Minneapolis

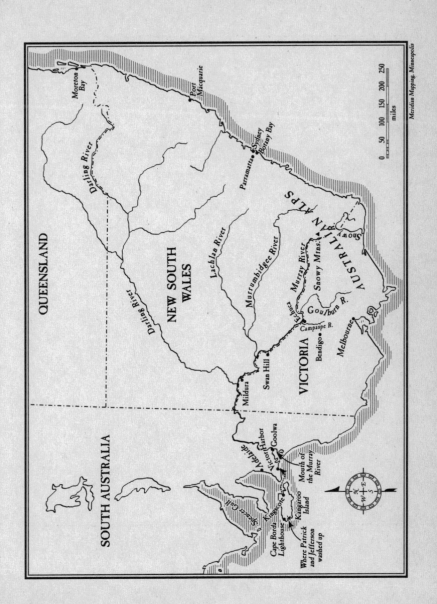

QUEENSLAND

Darling River

NEW SOUTH
WALES

Morton
Bay

Port
Macquaric

Darling River

Lachlan River

Murrumbidgee River

Parramatta Sydney
Bolany Bay

AUSTRALIAN ALPS

Snowy Mtns.

Snowy R.

Murray River

Echuca

Goulburn R.

Campaspe R.

Bendigo

Melbourne

VICTORIA

Swan Hill

Mildura

SOUTH AUSTRALIA

Spencer Gulf

Adelaide

Kingscote

Victor Harbor

Goolwa

Mouth of
the Murray
River

Kangaroo
Island

Cape Borda
Lighthouse

Where Patrick
and Jefferson
washed up

miles

0 50 100 150 200 250

Meridian Mapping, Minneapolis

CHAPTER 1

TIGHTROPE TROUBLE

Patrick McWaid closed his eyes, but it only made his stomach feel worse. He gripped the sides of the tiny wooden wheelbarrow and tried not to look at the river twenty feet below, wondering how he had been talked into being pushed across the Murray River on a tightrope.

"Sit still, kid!" The Great Philippe commanded him.

Patrick looked over his shoulder to see the man waving at the crowds gathered on both sides of the Murray. Most were on the Echuca side, and it seemed as if the entire pioneer town had rushed down to the waterfront for the afternoon entertainment. After all, acrobats and performers didn't get to this corner of Australia very often in 1868—especially not in June, when the rains came.

Ahead of them, the tightrope was stretched from the Echuca wharf—a high, wooden structure built to handle a dozen paddle steamers, as well as the river's ups and downs. His family's floating home was there, too—the *Lady Elisabeth*, a little steamer that belonged to Patrick's grandfather. They had been staying there for the past few days to help their grandfather prepare for another of his trips up the river.

The other end of the tightrope was tied fast to a tall eucalyptus tree on the Moama side. Moama was a smaller settlement of rough shacks and crooked little wooden buildings on the other side of the river that Patrick's grandfather said hardly amounted to anything.

"I said, sit still!" ordered The Great Philippe as they teetered from side to side. "Or do you want me to dump you into your river?" Patrick looked back again, and the man's eye twitched nervously. Philippe blew out hard, and Patrick could smell the chalky powder the man had dusted on his hands and feet so he wouldn't slip.

"Sorry," whispered Patrick. He hunched down but glanced back to see the sweat drip down the man's eyebrow. "What happened to your French accent?"

"I knew I should have gotten someone else," mumbled the tightrope walker, taking a few more steps and pausing for balance. "Instead of a little Scottish boy who asks too many questions."

"I'm Irish. And I'm twelve already." Patrick wasn't sure the man would understand him, his teeth were chattering so much, but he wasn't going to let someone call him Scottish.

"Irish, Scottish, whatever. Back home in Philly it's all the same. Just sit up straight, will you? People need to see your red hair so they know there's someone in the wheelbarrow and not just a sack of potatoes."

Patrick took a deep breath and tried to put his head up, but by that time his stomach wouldn't let him. Nothing seemed to be working the way it was supposed to. He couldn't tell his teeth to stop chattering or his hands to stop shivering, and he couldn't even tell his head to turn the way he wanted it to.

"I-I'm trying."

As The Great Philippe inched forward, Patrick slowly forced himself to look ahead at the crowd on the Echuca wharf, which seemed to be swaying just as much as they were. He couldn't make out the nut-brown hair of his fifteen-year-old sister, Becky, and he couldn't see his mother, either. Petite like her daughter, she wouldn't stand above the crowd anyway. Patrick's grandfather— everyone called him the "Old Man"—also wasn't anywhere in sight.

Maybe they're not there after all, he hoped. *Because if Ma sees me up here . . .*

Patrick tried not to imagine what his mother would say about the stunt as he squeezed his eyes shut. All the swaying was making him queasy, and he couldn't catch his breath. He regretted very much having eaten lunch just before climbing into the wheelbarrow.

"I think I'm going to be sick," Patrick finally announced, feeling his stomach turn inside out. He clapped a hand to his mouth but tried not to jerk his head.

"Hey! Don't do that! Do you hear me?" The Great Philippe swung a leg out for balance and the wheelbarrow rocked dangerously—which of course only made things worse for Patrick's churning stomach. Patrick gripped his knees, shut his eyes, buried his face under his arms, and waited for the impact of their high dive into the river. His head spun.

I'm going to die, he thought, and he wasn't sure if it was going to be from falling or just getting sick on the high wire. Either way . . .

"I'm sorry." Patrick just wanted the wheelbarrow to stop swaying. He made the mistake of looking back once more to see The Great Philippe struggling for balance. "I'm very sorry."

"I've . . . never had . . ." Philippe mumbled under his breath, "a wheelbarrow rider . . . who got sick. You are not going to be the first."

"I don't want to be." Patrick heard the collected "ooh" and "ahh" of the people on both sides of the river, then wild applause grew louder as they swung dangerously. He glimpsed the river below every time they swung one way or the other.

"Hold on, kid. We're almost there. Just a few feet."

Patrick peeked up through his arms and dug his fingernails into the side of the wheelbarrow. By this time Patrick could hear a brass band playing a marching tune, and the applause grew louder as Philippe ran the last few feet up to the waiting safety of the wharf.

"Dank you, *madames et messieurs*!" shouted the man. "*Merci*. Dank you." The Great Philippe dumped Patrick unceremoniously onto the hard wooden boards of the Echuca wharf, where he lay on his back, panting and staring up at a crowd of clapping people. The performer was smiling and waving as the band played a victory march.

"Get up, kid," Philippe whispered through his teeth as he waved to the crowd and kicked at Patrick's side with his ballet slippers. Someone else hoisted Patrick to his feet. His friend Jack Duggan.

"That was great, Patrick." Jack, who was a year or two older than Patrick and at least half a head taller, still wore a summer tan that seemed to make his freckles pop out all the more. He pounded Patrick on the back and held Patrick's hand up like a winning boxer. "Now, aren't you glad I talked you into this?"

Patrick choked and tried to pull his hand back down, but Jack was too strong. He looked around at the crowd but still couldn't find his mother, sister, or grandfather.

"I thought I was going to die out there."

Jack turned to The Great Philippe, who was still bowing and twirling the ends of his handlebar moustache as the applause died down. "He was great, wasn't he? I told you my friend would be great."

Patrick studied his shoes as Philippe stared at him. His head was still spinning, and his stomach felt as if it were still out over the river.

"I was *magnifique*, as always." The performer beamed. "And how many in your family, boy?"

"Five." Patrick wasn't sure why the man asked. "I mean four. My father . . . he's not, um, here right now."

"*Oui*, but of course. Here are five tickets to our circus, and you bring your friend, *non*?"

Patrick paused and looked up. "Thanks, but I thought you said you'd give me a shilling if I—"

"A shilling?" The Great Philippe laughed. "No, no, no. Perhaps you misunderstood. But of course this is far better than money, non?"

For a moment Patrick felt his ears heat up in anger. He'd been tricked, and there was nothing he could do about it. The man *had* promised to pay him for riding in the wheelbarrow.

"But you said—"

Jack nudged him in the side. "Take the tickets, Patrick," he whispered. "Everybody's looking at us."

Jack was right. The Great Philippe smiled his stage smile and held out a handful of crumpled circus tickets. Patrick sighed.

"Enjoy the show." The high-wire artist bowed and turned back to the audience to shake more hands.

"So let's see the tickets," said Jack. "They're for the big show, right?"

They could barely read the name, *The Great Australian Traveling Circus, Main Show*. Someone had crossed out the date and written in a new one: *Friday, June 5, 1868*.

"Day after tomorrow," said Patrick. "Think your parents will let you come?"

Jack shrugged. "You know I've been working a lot at the boatyard with my father lately."

"That's why you don't go to school much, right?"

"You and your sister haven't even been at all."

"We will tomorrow. First time. But the tickets are for seven o'clock on Friday night."

"I still don't know if I can come," said Jack.

Meanwhile, The Great Philippe stood up in his wheelbarrow for a better view over the crowd. "Ladies and gentlemen, this was only de . . . how do you say it . . . de 'warm-up.'" He paused to see who was still listening. "Tonight, as part of the celebration to welcome the rest of my circus and His Majesty Prince Alfred, duke of Edinburgh, you shall see an even greater feat on dis rope—a human fireworks display! An even more fantastic . . ."

Patrick and Jack slipped through the crowd as Philippe went on with his speech. They hurried past the brick warehouses that lined the waterfront, skipping High Street and turning right, away from town. Only a couple of blocks wide, this was where the smaller Campaspe River almost emptied into the larger Murray River, but then seemed to change its mind and go its own way for another mile or two, in a roundabout way. The aborigine people who had first lived there called the area Echuca, *where the waters meet* in their language, and that was how the town got its name. But Jack called the marshy area north of town "the Peninsula" because of the rivers running on three of its sides. Without any houses and dotted with eucalyptus or "gum" trees, it was a perfect place for setting up circus tents—as long as the river didn't keep rising.

"What's your rush, Patrick? Don't you want to hear more about the prince coming?"

"I already know all about it." Patrick frowned. "Half the town's going to be down at the train station. But you heard Philippe, didn't you? He said he was going to give a shilling to anyone who sat in his wheelbarrow."

Jack just shrugged. "Maybe he did. But the tickets—"

"I can't give my ma circus tickets for her birthday. It's today. I was going to buy her something."

"What's wrong with circus tickets?"

"I can't just give her *that*. I don't even think she approves of that kind of thing. And if she knew . . ." Patrick's voice trailed off when he heard someone calling his name.

"I better go," said Jack. "Maybe I'll see you Friday."

"If I survive that long," answered Patrick.

Jack took a trail that looped around to the right, back toward the Murray and behind a couple of ramshackle cabins.

"Patrick Ian McWaid!" Sarah McWaid came up behind him a moment later with a firm grip on his shoulder. Her hands were small and almost delicate looking, but strong and used to work. With her left eyebrow raised, her lips pressed tightly together, and the fire in her Irish eyes, Patrick knew what was coming.

"I heard just now there was a redheaded boy taken across the river and back, and in a wheelbarrow, yet. You wouldn't know anything about that, now, would you?"

"Um . . ." Patrick swallowed hard and tried to think of something to say. "The tightrope walker's name was The Great Philippe. He was pretending to be French, like that Blondin fellow I read about in the newspaper, who walked across Niagara Falls in America, only—"

"You know precisely what I'm talking about, Patrick." She stepped around to face him squarely. "How could you do such a thing?"

"I wasn't going to, but he promised he would pay me." Patrick dug his hand into his pocket and came out with the tickets. "Only this is what I got instead. Happy birthday."

Mrs. McWaid shook her head slowly. "Patrick, I cannot keep watch over you alone anymore. Ever since your father was . . ." She took a deep breath, and her shoulders sagged. Patrick knew she didn't want to talk about the past year of their lives. After his father, John McWaid, had been convicted back in Ireland of a crime he never committed, nothing had been the same for them as a family. First the long trip to Australia, where his father had been taken to a prison colony. Then the news that Pa had escaped, and that Conrad Burke, who used to be his father's boss, was trying to kill him. As far as Patrick could tell, his father was the only one who knew the truth about the real criminal—the police commissioner Burke was trying so hard to protect. Burke had been sent to Australia to make sure Mr. McWaid would never tell what he knew. And now Patrick's father was still missing. So was Conrad Burke.

"For a fact," his mother found her voice again, "you promised me you would behave yourself while your father's gone. This is the way you keep your promises?"

"No, Ma. I'm sorry. . . ."

"Patrick, I don't want you to get hurt—or worse. You and Becky and Michael are all I have now."

Shouting and whistling in the distance caught their attention. By the sound of it, there were several riders headed toward Echuca.

"Look at that!" shouted a young boy running toward the riders. "They're bringing in the escaped prisoner!"

CHAPTER 2

TIGER BY THE TAIL

Patrick was almost afraid to look at the men coming down the trail, rough-looking men with bird's nest beards who appeared as if they probably hadn't seen a bath in months. Halfway down the line rode a man with his wrists tied behind his back, his head covered by a wide-brimmed hat pulled low over his ears. Patrick tried to get closer, but the horses trotted quickly past.

"Ma!" Patrick called back to his mother, who was looking on with a troubled expression on her face. "Could you see?"

His mother shook her head, and Patrick knew it would be up to him to find out.

What if it's Pa? he asked himself. *What if they finally caught him?*

Part of him didn't want to know, but still he ran toward the crowd for a better look.

"Who is it?"

"Heard it's that McWaid fellow," said a man. By that time they had dragged the unfortunate prisoner off his horse and pulled him through the crowd into the jailhouse.

"Who told you that?" asked Patrick. He still hadn't been able to get a good look at the prisoner.

"That's what I hear, is all."

Patrick pushed his way through the crowd, trying to inch

closer, trying to hear anything the men were saying on the front steps of the jailhouse. Constable Alexander Fitzgerald had appeared for only a moment, then disappeared back into the building. A couple of the men who had come riding in with the prisoner stood out on the veranda, obviously not happy.

"He's your man," grumbled one. "Looks just like the poster said. Now, I'll be waiting for my payment, see?"

"If it's him, you'll get your money," replied a uniformed man as he fought to keep the crowds back. Patrick had seen him before with Constable Fitzgerald. He was younger than the other constable, with big, strong arms and ruddy cheeks. He raised his hands for attention.

"Now, people, you've got to back away. For your own safety, please. There's not enough room for all of you. In fact, why don't you all just go home? You can read about what happened in the newspaper."

"Come on, Mitchell," shouted someone from the crowd. "We want to know now."

"You'll find out soon enough," Constable Mitchell answered. "But first you've got to give us some breathing room."

A few people in the crowd groaned in disappointment, but most of the people listened to the constable and started to drift away.

Now I can slip through, Patrick thought to himself as he ducked around knots of people. Crouching low, he weaved his way through the crowd, closer to the front.

"Excuse me," he repeated, over and over. "Excuse me, please."

Patrick wasn't sure where he was going or what he was going to do when he got there. All he knew was that if his father was in the building in front of him, he was going to see him.

With his heart beating wildly, Patrick scooted around a wide man to find himself at the front of the crowd, almost face-to-face with the assistant constable. The young man was still waving his arms and trying to get rid of the people.

"Pardon me," began Patrick. Constable Mitchell didn't look up, just kept shouting at the crowd.

"Hello?" Patrick raised his voice until the constable finally looked down.

"Back, please," the constable told him. Instead, Patrick took a step forward.

"I have to get inside," announced Patrick.

Mitchell only crossed his big arms and shook his head. "No one is going in there right now. Not until McWaid is taken care of."

Patrick gasped. "So it *is* John McWaid?"

The deputy grunted. "Matches the description is what I hear. Red hair. Skinny. Says he's someone else, of course."

"I can tell you if he is."

The constable looked down at Patrick with a frown.

"Our problem right now isn't identifying this man. It's keeping him away from these good people." He looked out over the crowd with a disgusted expression.

"This is the convict who stole some of my best cows!" yelled someone in the crowd, a man who didn't look as if he was interested in moving along. "What are you going to do about it?"

Mitchell put out his hands again in an effort to calm the men down. "Look, Mr. Harris, we let you do your job, so you just let us do ours. We're going to make sure things are put right."

"Yeh, right for who?" demanded Harris. "You're going to ship him off to Melbourne, and we'll never see him again. What about me cows, then?"

"Why don't you just bring him back out here, Constable?" yelled another man. "We'll take care of him for you! Save you the trouble."

Patrick's spine tingled at the laughs of the men around him. And for a moment he thought he saw fear in the constable's face.

"So what about it, Constable?" challenged Harris. "Are you going to bring the gully raker out or not?"

The constable's face turned red, and he pushed past a couple of people to face the heckler nose to nose.

"That's not the way we do things around here, Jed, and you know it. We don't even know for certain that he *is* McWaid, or a cattle rustler, like you say. Now, go home or I'll throw you in jail, too, for starting a riot. Is that what you want?"

The man pulled his chin back and muttered something Patrick couldn't hear. Some of the people around the pair chuckled.

"Better go home, Jed," said one.

"Bah," snarled the man as he turned away.

Patrick had been pushed up to the front door of the jail, and no one else seemed to notice when the tall door opened just a few inches. A face appeared at the top of the door, probably checking to make sure if Mitchell was all right. Before anyone noticed, Patrick slipped inside, past Constable Fitzgerald.

"Hey, you!" yelled Fitzgerald. His voice echoed when the front door slammed shut. "What do you think you're doing in here?"

The city's jail wasn't large, with only six cells in the back of a single room and a couple of desks in front. The first few cells looked empty. Patrick darted to the next one, where a little round man was slumped on a bench, sleeping.

The constable grabbed him from behind, but Patrick whirled to face him.

"Please, sir, I must see my father!"

Patrick wiggled free to sprint down the short hallway, checking both sides. In the last cell on the left, a man with a sparse reddish beard lunged at him, grabbing hold of the front of Patrick's shirt and pulling his face to the bars. Terrified, Patrick tried to resist, but the man in the cell only held on more tightly. All Patrick could see at such a close range was the man's enormous eyes, bloodshot and wild like a captured animal's—but there was something horribly familiar about him.

"They've got the wrong man!" insisted the prisoner, inches from Patrick's face. His breath assaulted Patrick like a fist. "Can't they see? I almost had him, and they captured me instead!"

Constable Fitzgerald yanked Patrick from behind in a desperate tug-of-war with the prisoner.

"Let the boy go!" he ordered.

CHAPTER 3

BUSHRANGER'S DEAL

For a moment Patrick was lifted off his feet between the two struggling men. He turned his face to avoid the stench of the prisoner's foul breath.

"No!" insisted the wild-eyed prisoner.

As the front of his shirt nearly ripped in two, Patrick broke free, falling back against Constable Fitzgerald on the other side of the narrow hallway. For the first time he took a good look at the prisoner the crowd had thought was John McWaid. But aside from the red beard, Patrick saw nothing that reminded him of his father— only a boy in his teens with a desperate face, dirty and scratched, as if he had just run from a battle. His clothes were mud-caked and torn, and there were black circles under his eyes, which narrowed as he stared at Patrick.

"I know you," said the prisoner, reaching out his hand as if he would grab Patrick once more. "You're that kid, that lousy kid who caused us so much grief."

Patrick closed his eyes, wishing he had never pushed his way into the jail. Not for this.

"See? He knows me!" The prisoner laughed. "We spent some time together a few weeks back, didn't we?"

Patrick backed away, back down the hall. That was an adventure he preferred not to remember—he and his sister, Becky, had been taken prisoner by a group of outlaw bushrangers, all hired by Burke to find his father.

"Hey, don't leave now, kid. I thought you were coming for a visit. Matter of fact, I can tell you where to find your father, only not from the inside of this cell. How about it, Constable? Want to make a deal?"

The constable held on to Patrick's arm. "Who is this fellow?" he asked.

"Billy Simpson," Patrick whispered. "His brother is Hookey Simpson, the bushranger who just went to trial. He was one of the men in the gang that kidnapped my sister and me a month ago."

The constable whistled. "Well, now, that's different."

"Sure it's different." The prisoner strutted back and forth in his cell. "And I have something you want."

"What's that?"

"I can tell you exactly where to find John McWaid, the escaped prisoner you're looking for."

"Did you find him?" asked Patrick, taking a step back toward Simpson.

The prisoner smiled. "Sure did. We were watching his hideout when your friends out there jumped us." He pointed in the direction of the street.

" 'We'? 'Us'?" wondered the constable. "Who's us?"

Simpson smiled. "Not so fast, Constable. I'll tell you what you want to know, but you're going to have to give a little. I was the only one the boys here were able to grab."

"They should have captured all of your gang," said Patrick.

The prisoner held up his hands and smiled. "For what? Only thing I've done wrong is have an older brother who's a famous outlaw. And now I can help you capture a wanted man. What do you say?"

"He's lying," said Patrick. "He was part of a gang that robbed a stagecoach. The Cobb and Company drivers can identify him. My sister and I saw him, too."

"Oh, come on, Constable." Simpson put out his hand. "Do I look like a lawbreaker to you? Me and me mates were just being good citizens and following the trail of this John McWaid fellow, same as you. Nothing wrong with that, is there? I can tell you right where he is—only he's going to be gone if you wait."

The constable rubbed his bearded chin, as if he was thinking about the offer.

"You can't do it," Patrick urged him. "All he wants to do is get out of jail. He's not going to tell you the truth."

Simpson laughed. "Look at that, will you? You know, Constable, that the man we're talking about is this boy's father, don't you? That explains a few things, eh?"

"You're not telling me anything I didn't already know." Constable Fitzgerald looked at Patrick and frowned.

"Of course, I don't blame him. No, not a bit," continued Simpson. "Like I said, I know what it's like being related to a famous outlaw."

Patrick could still hear the rest of the crowd outside the jail, hooting and whistling. Maybe it was another speech about hanging John McWaid.

"Well, Constable, what'll it be?" Simpson sounded as if he were a lawyer in a courtroom, arguing his case. "You have no right to keep me locked up like this, seeing as how I'm not the man you're looking for. Even the kid can tell you that."

"But he's one of the Simpson gang," insisted Patrick. He had the sinking feeling that the constable was about to free Billy Simpson. "My grandfather can tell you as much. So can Mr. Duggan. This man should be in jail."

"And for what?" Simpson raised his voice. "If being related to an outlaw is a crime, then throw the kid in here with me right now, Constable. Otherwise, let me go free. And don't forget, the first thing I'll do when I'm out is take you to capture your *real* prisoner. Isn't *that* going to look good in the newspapers? 'Heroic Constable Captures Escaped Prisoner.' Come on, now, what do you say?"

Constable Fitzgerald rocked back on his heels, still thinking, when the front door opened and Mitchell poked his head inside.

"You all right in there, Alex?" he asked.

Constable Fitzgerald nodded and led Patrick to the door.

"Fine," replied the constable. "Mitch, see that this young fellow doesn't come back in here, will you?"

"But, Constable—" Patrick tried, but the men wouldn't let him finish.

"Out with you now, boy," Constable Fitzgerald told him. "You've done enough already."

Several people in the crowd stared curiously at Patrick while Constable Fitzgerald whispered something into the other constable's ear.

Mitchell's eyes grew wide, and he looked down at Patrick. "You're sure of it?"

Fitzgerald nodded. "Explain it to everybody out here."

"Folks?" Mitchell whistled loudly through his teeth, and the crowd hushed. Patrick took the chance to slip into the crowd. "Listen. Constable Fitzgerald has just informed me that the prisoner has been identified, and he is *not* the escaped convict we were looking for."

The crowd groaned as Mitchell went on.

"I repeat, he is *not* John McWaid. However, we have good information about the prisoner's whereabouts, and Constable Fitzgerald and I expect to have him in custody within forty-eight hours."

Patrick ducked back to the other side of the street where it was clear, and his mother came rushing up to him.

"Patrick! Where have you been? And what happened to your shirt?"

Patrick looked down at his torn blue shirt. "It's not Pa," he finally told her.

"I heard. But do they know who it really is?"

Patrick nodded again and closed his eyes. "They know."

He could still smell Billy Simpson's breath in his face, and it made him shiver. And he wasn't quite sure if he was relieved or disappointed not to find his father in a jail cell.

Mrs. McWaid crossed her arms as they walked.

"Be that as it may, Patrick, you've got to listen to me now."

Patrick dragged his feet as they made their way back to the wharf.

"Are you listening?" She put her hand on his arm. "I want you to stay with your sister this time and not go wandering off by yourself. I still have a few more things to get for your grandfather before he has to leave. And we'll be having dinner shortly."

"Yes, Ma." Patrick kicked a pebble into the river as hard as he could, thinking about how Billy Simpson was getting out of prison, and what might happen to his father. It wasn't fair! How could the constable let him go?

"Michael, get down from there," Patrick's mother scolded his eight-year-old brother, Michael, who was balancing on the side railing of their grandfather's paddle steamer. "I don't want to have to tell you again."

"But, Ma," protested Michael. "I'm just practicing for my show, 'Michael McWaid and His Wild Animal Show.' Thrills! Trapeze artists! Fireworks!"

Michael teetered on the railing, and Patrick grabbed him by the legs, wrestling him down to the deck.

"What was all the noise up there in town, Patrick? Did you see what was going on?"

"I saw."

When Patrick didn't explain, Michael turned his attention to the out-of-tune brass band playing on the wharf, just below where The Great Philippe was getting ready to put on another show.

"What's wrong with you, Patrick?" asked Michael. "Don't you want to see the fireworks?"

Patrick shook his head. "Believe me, I've seen enough of The Great Philippe already."

After dinner when the shadows started to stretch into dusk, Patrick wandered around to the river side of the *Lady E*, away from the head-on screech of the trumpets and trombones. He picked up a rusty nail from the deck and threw it as hard as he could.

If Billy Simpson said he almost had him, he thought, looking across the river at two campfires, *Pa has to be somewhere close by*.

Patrick watched the rising river slowly surging by, trying to think of what to do. Rains from the past few weeks would push up the waters, but people from around town told him that generally the worst floods held off until the spring. This year had been wetter than usual, though—much wetter.

He heard a gentle thumping against the hull and looked down to see the ship's rowboat, left there by one of the crew. Without thinking much of it, he slipped over the side and sat in the rowboat.

"Are you sick?" his sister, Becky, asked from the deck above.

Patrick didn't answer right away. "Not at all. I'm fine."

"Well, you don't look it. You look horrible."

"Thank you very much, Dr. McWaid." Patrick splashed at the muddy brown water with one of the oars.

"The Great Philippe is going to go out over the river again."

"I've already seen him."

"But you haven't seen him with the fireworks. And Prince Alfred is supposed to arrive at the train station tonight, too."

"Hmm."

Becky stepped down into the back end of the rowboat but didn't say anything else. They had a perfect view of the tightrope and the wharf, as well as the river all the way down to Hopwood's Landing— where Henry Hopwood ran a ferry service back and forth across the river. Patrick had learned it was Mr. Hopwood who had actually founded Echuca.

Tonight, though, it looked as if Mr. Henry Hopwood had tied up his ferry. Patrick guessed that he, too, was watching the show.

"You know some men brought a prisoner into town today," he finally told his sister.

"I know. Someone they caught out in the bush."

Patrick nodded. "Everyone thought it was Pa."

"Is that a fact? But it wasn't, of course."

"How did you know?"

"Ma told me. But she didn't say who it really was."

"Billy Simpson. Can you believe it?"

Becky didn't say anything, just caught her breath.

"He told Constable Fitzgerald he would take him to where Pa was hiding—if they let him go."

"They're not going to do that, are they? Simpson is an outlaw! Grandpa could tell them as much."

"I tried to tell them that, but the constable doesn't seem to care. Last I heard, Simpson was doing a fair job of working a bargain with him."

Becky groaned. "At least Pa is still out there somewhere."

Patrick bit his lip as he rested on the oar and let the river wash through his fingers.

"There's just one thing to do," he began.

"I'm not sure I want to hear it, Patrick McWaid."

"I'm going to go see if I can talk to Billy Simpson again. Could be he would tell me where he saw Pa."

"You're daft, Patrick. That's absolutely crazy."

Patrick knew it sounded silly, but he couldn't think of anything else to do.

"Well, if nobody else is going to do anything about it, it's up to me."

"It is *not* up to you. You always act as if the world sits on your shoulders, as if you're the only one who can ever do anything."

Patrick brushed off his sister's comment.

"I'm still going to try."

"He's not going to talk to you," Becky said. "Why would he?"

"I haven't figured that part out yet."

"Even if he did, what would you do? Hide out with Pa?"

"Something like that. I'd go find Pa, and then I'd hide him."

"Oh, Patrick," Becky sighed. "Not again."

"Becky—" He started to protest, but he knew his sister was right.

"Becky what?" She took a deep breath. "We've talked about this so many times that I can't talk about it anymore. You're always saying that *we're* going to make it happen. *We're* in control. Well, that's not the way it really is, Patrick. And since you never say anything about trusting that *God* is in control, I don't even know if you believe that anymore."

The words stung, and Patrick smacked the water with his paddle. The crowd up on the wharf started to cheer as The Great Philippe stepped up on a platform and started waving his arms. Patrick couldn't make out all that he was saying, but some of the man's words drifted out across the water . . . "death-defying" . . . *"fantastique"* . . .

"See?" Becky spoke up again. "You're just like The Great whatever-his-name-is. A one-man show."

"All right, all right. I hear what you're saying." Patrick frowned as the twilight grew darker. "So are you saying it's useless, that we shouldn't be doing *anything*?

"We used to do much more than we do now," Becky answered after a few moments. Her quiet voice was nearly swallowed up by the cheers of the crowd.

"I don't understand."

"Think about it, Patrick."

"Don't play games. Just tell me."

The Great Philippe shouted something else, and the crowd clapped.

"Look at that crazy man," said Becky, obviously trying to change the subject. "What is he carrying?"

Surrounded by a hundred flickering lanterns, Philippe was walking out onto his tightrope again, this time holding a long balancing pole—with something strapped to both ends.

"Don't change the subject, Becky. Tell me."

She leaned forward with her elbows on her knees and looked straight at her brother. "I wanted you to reckon for yourself. We used to *pray*, Patrick."

Patrick caught his breath, waiting for the rest of the sermon to hit him in the gut. It didn't come, but what she had told him was already enough. *I've forgotten to pray about Pa.*

In the distance they saw a little flame in the half darkness, like a match, then something like a sparkler as the tightrope walker lit the fuse to a bright collection of spinning Roman candles, sputtering spark-throwers, and loud firecrackers. The crowd caught its breath in a big "ahh" as the performer waved his long fireworks pole over the river.

"Isn't that pretty?" asked Becky.

The fireworks' bright reflection on the water lit a path for two approaching barges, towed in single file slowly up the river by a stout little paddle steamer. Patrick cleared his head with a shake, his sister's words still echoing in his head.

We used to pray.

"Patrick?"

"Are you going to preach at me anymore?" he asked.

Becky laughed. "I already tried to change the subject, but you wouldn't let me. Look, what are those boats coming up the river? See them?"

Patrick could barely make out the two barges, piled high with wagons and boxes, and the small paddle steamer struggling to pull its load.

"I think it's the Great Australian Traveling Circus," explained Patrick. "And look! Philippe said he was going to light his fireworks while he's walking the rope. They're supposed to light the way."

"Looks more like he's trying to kill himself." Becky stood up to get a better view, and the boat rocked dangerously. "Listen!"

Patrick winced, then covered his ears. "All I hear are the fireworks."

"No, I'm talking about the circus animals."

"Did you hear that?" Their little brother stepped out of the second-story wheelhouse, from where their grandfather steered the *Lady Elisabeth*.

"Where did you come from?" Patrick wanted to know as he looked up at Michael.

"I was here all the time. Did you hear that elephant?"

"I'm not certain I know what an elephant sounds like."

"I don't, either," replied Michael. "But if I ever heard one, that's what I think it would sound like."

This time Patrick heard what Becky and Michael had talked

about: a long, trumpeting call—no, several different calls, then a deep, husky roar.

"Sounds like a lion," guessed Patrick.

Michael shook his head as he came down the ladder to join them. "This circus doesn't have lions. It must be a tiger."

"How do you know so much about this circus?" asked Patrick.

"I read the posters in town. A giant tent that holds four hundred and fifty people! Three ferocious tigers, including the rare, famous blue-eyed white tiger! The parade of elephants! And the bearded Madame Leotard, as large as four—"

"All right, Michael," interrupted Becky, stopping his wild gestures. "We understand."

"But didn't you read the posters? There's a big picture of a tiger with his mouth open like this—"

Michael demonstrated his best tiger-sized roar, and Becky shook her head. "Ma and I have been too busy."

"Look!" Michael pointed beyond the fireworks. The Great Philippe was making his way back to shore. "It's them—the circus animals."

Sure enough, the circus barges had come up the river, but the flashing light of the fireworks made it clear that something was wrong. They heard a crash and a splintering of wood. Then a scream—Patrick wasn't sure if it was a person or a circus animal.

He sat up straight and leaned closer. "Looks like the barges ran into each other! And isn't one of the barges tipping?"

Even above the crowd they could hear more voices.

"No, no, no," shouted one man from the barges. "You don't just open the cages! Not yet!"

"But we can't let them drown!" replied another man. The way their voices traveled over the water, it sounded as if they were standing right next to Patrick and Becky.

"Can't you see we're tipping over?" cried another man. "Stop the paddle steamer! And hold on to those animals!"

CHAPTER 4

Collision With Jumbo

In the confusion of the sinking barges, Becky was already untying the rope to their little boat.

"Where are you going?" asked Michael, scrambling down toward them. "Can I go, too?"

He didn't wait for an answer, only dove into the middle of the boat, nearly tipping it over.

"No, Michael!" Patrick stood up, but the river only sloshed over the side of the boat. Becky grabbed them both.

"Sit still, you two." She traded places with Michael and slipped the oars into place. "We're just going to see what's happening over there."

Patrick kept watch in the front of the boat; by that time, the river had turned into a screaming zoo. As they passed under The Great Philippe, another rocket went off, but instead of shooting up, it headed straight toward them.

"Watch out!" cried Becky, and the boys ducked for cover. The rocket fizzled out with a mighty splash only inches from their boat.

Patrick looked up to see Philippe teetering, then losing his balance.

"Oh no." Patrick's eyes grew wide in horror. "Here he comes!"

Philippe hit the water behind them with a mighty cannonball splash. His balance pole speared the water safely off to the side.

"Is he all right?" asked Becky as the tightrope walker came to the surface sputtering and splashing. He ignored them and struck out for the far shore, away from the crowd.

"I think so," answered Patrick quietly. "But he's not wanting to chat just now."

Becky rowed them slowly toward the crippled barges. The closer they got, the more the water was alive with animals.

"Look over there!" said Michael, pointing at the dark shape of the first barge. The deck had just slipped under the water, and a man from the paddle steamer was on deck, wrestling with cages. The air was filled with the shrieks of frightened animals and the shouts of more men from the other barge.

"The weight is pulling the other one down, too!" Patrick stared at the second barge, piled high with animals and boxes, still floating, but also tipping dangerously to the side. Several of the men were cutting a team of horses loose. From the first barge, completely awash, two enormous shapes like boulders seemed to roll into the water and float directly toward them.

"Becky!" cried Patrick, grabbing one of the oars. "We're too close!"

Suddenly a huge snake landed squarely in Patrick's lap. A thump knocked the boat almost on its side, where it scooped up gallons of river water before righting itself. The snake—or whatever it was—gave a *puff* and slipped back into the river. Patrick jumped out of his seat and grabbed the side of the boat, hoping to keep them stable. There was no way he wanted to fall into that water.

"Hold on!" yelled Becky. "An elephant just rammed into us!"

Even though the animal was close up, Patrick still wasn't sure what he was seeing. The huge creature at their side was breathing hard, and it struggled as if it wanted to climb into the boat with them.

Another animal joined the first, trumpeting into the darkness. Michael leaned over the back of the boat and patted its enormous head.

"You're all right," he told it, stroking its head as if it were a big gray dog. Something else—a huge cat, maybe—shrieked in the distance.

Patrick shivered at the sound. "What was that?" He listened carefully, but no more shrieks came—only the sound of their grandfather's commanding voice that cut like a knife through the noise.

"Patrick!"

"That's Grandpa," answered Becky, rowing hard. The cat shrieked again—or growled.

"No, I mean the animal." Patrick scanned the water around them, but he couldn't see anything that looked like a cat. Several of the men from the circus barge shouted something in their direction just as the water around them turned to foam with the thrashing of the elephants. Patrick couldn't tell how many surrounded them: three, four, five?

"Row to shore, Becky," suggested Michael. "Maybe they'll follow us."

"Michael's right." Patrick held on. "If we don't do something fast, these animals are going to sink us the same way they did their barge."

Michael kept patting the closest elephant on the head. "Come on, Jumbo. Follow us. You'll be fine."

"Watch out, Becky!" warned Patrick from the front of the boat. "We almost ran into a white horse."

Becky rowed as quickly as she could for the shore just past Hopwood's Landing. But with all the animals in the water, the best they could manage was a crazy, zigzag course.

Several yellow lanterns were now waving on the shore, and they heard their mother calling them. As far as Patrick could tell, the crowd that had been watching the fireworks from the wharf had moved to the marshy waterfront by Hopwood's Landing, closer to the Peninsula.

The elephants were able to touch bottom several boat lengths before they made the shore, and they tottered uncertainly in the mud. By the time they made it to the circle of light from the crowd's lanterns, Patrick could tell they had three elephants in tow: a baby and two larger ones.

"I think this is the mama." Michael pointed out one of the larger ones, the one that seemed to watch over the smallest. The crowd on the shore backed up respectfully as the three animals slogged through the mud, still breathing hard and looking warily at their audience.

"Give them some room!" shouted Michael, hopping out of the boat into the mud. The little elephant, though he was obviously only a baby compared to the other two animals, still stood far taller than Michael.

"No, Michael," warned Becky. "Stay away from the animals. They might be more dangerous on land."

Michael ignored his older sister. Still cooing to the elephants as he had done while they were out on the river, he tried to lead the huge animals through the noisy crowd. The mother elephant stood firm, though, guarding her young and waving her trunk as a warning.

"Stop!" ordered a voice from inside a covered carriage that pulled up in front of them. A few of the people pulled back from the new arrival as a tall, well-dressed man in a fine dark suit and a broad mustache stepped out to stand in front of them. The driver of the coach didn't have a chance to open the door for him.

"Is this the circus?" asked the mustached man in a fine, precise English accent. "I didn't know swimming elephants were part of the act."

"No, sir, they aren't. We just saw them in the river," Becky explained, "and we tried to help them—"

"No need to apologize, young lady." In the flickering lantern light, the man gazed in wonder at the elephants. "This young fellow seems to know how to handle them quite well."

"Are these your elephants?" Michael asked the man. "If they are, I wasn't trying to take them or anything."

The man with the mustache laughed. "Mine? No, son. Elephants are one thing I don't own. Although . . ."

He looked thoughtfully at the animals while a thin, nervous-looking man with a pen and a black leather notebook in hand came rushing to his side.

"Your Highness," barked the man with the notebook, "we can't linger here, or the welcoming crowd from the railroad station will follow us again. I've made arrangements for you at a local hotel. We're expected."

Your Highness? Patrick's jaw dropped when he realized he was standing in front of Prince Alfred, duke of Edinburgh.

"Forgive me." The prince put out his hand for Patrick to shake, the same way any other adult would have done. "Perhaps I'm too used to being announced. I'm Prince Alfred."

Patrick's throat clamped shut in fright as he shook the man's hand. He moved his lips, but no sound came out.

"I'm Michael McWaid," chirped Michael, quickly offering his own hand. "He's Patrick. And this is my sister, Becky—her real name is Rebecca. She's the one who rowed the boat so we could rescue the elephants. I'm going to have my own circus and call it 'Michael McWaid and His Wild Animal Show.' Do you want to see it when it's ready?"

Becky managed a red-faced curtsy as their mother came running up to them.

"Becky, what are you children—" began their mother, but she stopped short when she saw whom they were speaking to. "Oh, dear . . . Your Highness, I had no idea. . . ."

"Quite all right," answered Prince Alfred. "It's my fault for simply arriving like this, unannounced. I really shouldn't have, you see, but for all the commotion." He smiled pleasantly. "I'm afraid my curiosity got the better of me."

"I trust my children weren't disturbing—"

"They're fine, I assure you," he finished. "And it looks as if they've rescued several of the circus animals. Resourceful children you have here, Mrs. . . . McWaid, was it?"

"That's right." She reached for the boys and pulled them back toward her.

"Well, then, Mrs. McWaid, assuming the rest of the animals are rounded up, I presume we'll enjoy the performance as scheduled

Friday evening." He flashed them a pleasant smile. "Really, this is a highlight of my tour to the Australian colony."

"Your Highness—" the prince's aide tapped his notebook with his pencil and frowned, "we really shouldn't be here. We're late for our next reception."

"Yes, yes, Hugh. Always a schedule, even though I've lost track of the days. And tomorrow, where?"

"Tomorrow is Thursday, Your Majesty, and you'll be touring a sheep ranch. Then Friday you're meeting with another group of landowners, and the circus performance is back here in Echuca Friday night. . . ." His assistant's voice droned on as Prince Alfred nodded and disappeared back into his carriage.

In the meantime three or four circus men had reached the Peninsula to claim their elephants. They herded the animals toward a corral someone had roped between several trees.

"Well, at least it saves us the trouble of unloading all these beasts," said one, slapping a stick against one of the big elephants' back legs to direct her into the corral.

"Ha," said another. "I thought with those leaky barges we'd never make it as far as we did."

In the distance, there was the unmistakable snarl of a big cat.

"What's that sound, young man?" A woman holding a lantern stepped in front of one of the elephant handlers.

"Oh, that's one of the tigers, ma'am." The elephant man sounded as if he were talking about the weather. "Not to worry, though. They're all under control."

As the crowd thinned, Patrick tried to follow the elephant trainers, but his mother pulled him away.

"I sure hope you're right about the tigers," one of the men murmured to the trainer who had answered the woman's question. "I wouldn't like to think of what might happen if any of them escape."

The sound of yet another growl sent a shiver up Patrick's spine, and he thought of his father out in the bush. The growl seemed to come from farther upriver, farther away, but it was hard to tell. What if the man was wrong about the tigers? What if one of them had escaped?

CHAPTER 5

OUTLAW ON THE LOOSE

The clouds opened up again, sending the McWaids scurrying back to the wharf and the dry safety of the *Lady Elisabeth*. Patrick stopped as the others stepped aboard.

Becky looked back. "Come on, Patrick, we're getting all wet."

"No, you go ahead. Tell Ma I'll be back in just a few minutes."

"But you can't just wander around out there at night. Where are you going?"

"I'll be just a minute. Don't worry."

Patrick ran through the dark, rainy streets, happy not to see anyone else. He tried to keep to the plank sidewalks, but the mud seemed to be everywhere. His sister's words from earlier that evening came back to him. *"He's not going to talk to you. Why would he?"*

Maybe not, he told himself, slipping into the darkness behind the city jail. *But I still have to try. This is probably my only chance. If Billy Simpson really knows where Pa is, I have to know.*

He passed behind the Shamrock Hotel and noticed a pile of broken wooden crates piled at the back door.

These should work, he thought, taking an armload. It was too dark to see, but in the shadows he thought he heard someone pushing over a pile of rubbish, cast-off junk from the hotel. A pile of something came crashing down in the darkness, and a figure appeared at the dimly lit back door.

"Hey!" he yelled. All Patrick could make out was his white apron—probably the cook. "Get out of there! Shoo!"

Patrick backed up slowly and hugged the wall, out of sight. For a moment he thought he heard a low, deep snarl, but he wasn't sure. Actually, he felt it more than heard it. Patrick strained his eyes to see into the darkness behind the mess of garbage and crates.

"Anyone there?" he whispered, not really wanting to hear an answer. Something moved again, slowly, and then it was gone.

Must have been a dog, Patrick told himself as he hurried away, but he was too afraid to investigate. He didn't look back as he came around the block behind the city jail.

Which window? Patrick set down his crates and looked up at three identical windows on the backside of the building, each one set higher than he could reach, at least without a boost. Finally he chose the last one, stacking three boxes right underneath.

As he moved to step up, the boxes teetered and fell with a crash. Patrick slipped back into the deep shadows behind the building. Two dogs scampered past, one chasing the other. Neither seemed to notice Patrick.

All right, try again. He restacked the crates, and this time balanced himself against the jail's outside wall as he stepped up on his homemade ladder. It rocked a little but held. A moment later he was swaying on the top of three crates, trying to hold on to the bars of the tiny window.

Inside the jail, he could see a faint light from the front room. He could easily pick out the form of a man in the cell below.

"Simpson," he whispered. "Up here."

At first the man below him didn't move, and Patrick heard the scraping of a chair in the front room. Someone cleared his throat, and the front door cracked open. The man below looked up at the window.

"Huh?" he grunted, too loud for Patrick's comfort. The man sounded older than Billy Simpson. But it had to be the right cell.

"Shh!" whispered Patrick. "I came to find out where my father is. You must tell me."

The man said nothing for a minute.

"Please, you're the only one who can tell me where he is. If you're still stuck in jail, what does it hurt for you to tell me?"

The man mumbled something, and Patrick leaned his ear up to the window's cold metal bars to hear better.

"Pardon?" asked Patrick. "What did you say?"

"I said, I don't know who you are or what you're doing here, but unless you want to meet a constable, you'd better get on home in a hurry, kid."

Patrick's heart fell to his feet when he realized the man was not Billy Simpson. And he nearly fell over when someone cleared his throat behind him.

"Get down from there, boy," ordered Constable Mitchell in a loud voice. "Right now!"

Patrick turned to see the outline of the big young man standing behind him, with one hand on his hip and the other holding a lantern. From the tone of his command, Patrick had a pretty good idea the constable was not happy.

"Yes, sir." Patrick jumped down to the alleyway. "I'm sorry, sir. I can explain. You see, I was hoping to find Billy Simpson and—"

"Look, boy," interrupted Constable Mitchell. "I don't know what you were hoping to do here, but Simpson's gone."

"Gone?" squeaked Patrick. "Then what about Constable Fitzgerald?" He was afraid he already knew what Mitchell would say.

"Gone, too, for a while."

"Are they looking for John McWaid?" *I have to know* . . . he thought.

"That's not your business. Now, go home." Mitchell took Patrick by the arm and pulled him away from the building. "Before I decide to lock you up, too."

Patrick didn't ask any more questions, just ran as fast as he could through the quiet streets back to the wharf, taking a wide detour around the hotel where he had heard the snarling sound.

"*Think*, Patrick," he told himself when he finally stopped at the edge of town. "What can you do to help Pa?" He watched the dark, rainy river snake its way in silence past the tall, silvery-green eucalyptus trees. The almost minty smell of a sheltering eucalyptus tree made his nose tingle when he took a deep breath.

He tried not to think about what his sister had told him, about not doing everything himself. And he tried even harder not to think about the outlaw Billy Simpson and where the man was probably leading Constable Fitzgerald. But he couldn't keep the outlaw's face out of his mind.

"So Billy Simpson thinks he knows where Pa is, does he?" Patrick asked himself, stepping clear of a puddle. He sighed. "Well, if he does, he's probably going to get a pile of reward money for his hard work—as if he deserves it."

He tried to imagine his father hiding somewhere out in the darkness, maybe under a tree or curled up in a hollow log, wet and cold. His father, who had never done anything to deserve a prison sentence in Australia. He had just been doing his job as a newspaper reporter back home in Ireland when he found out about the double life of a crooked police commissioner—a commissioner who had been paid off by criminals. . . .

"Only Pa and Burke know for sure what that terrible man did. But why did they have to blame it on Pa?"

He couldn't shake the feeling that everything he knew had been turned upside down in this strange new country. And not just the seasons, where winter was summer and fall was spring. The people who were supposed to help them didn't, while criminals got away with lie after lie. Wrong had turned into right, and right—well, Patrick was having a hard time finding it.

Patrick stomped in the puddle as hard as he could, not caring anymore if he was wet or dry.

"I'm sorry, Pa," he whispered into the darkness, as if his father could hear him. He tried to wipe his dripping nose, but his sleeve was soaking, too. "I'm glad you escaped, but they're about to find you again. And I can't do anything about it."

He fell to his knees, and his sobs turned into a prayer. For his father, mostly, but also for anyone else he could think of. For his sister, Becky, and his little brother, Michael. For their friends the Duggans, especially Jack, who was always having to work with his father at the boatyard. And then for his mother. He had caught her crying more than once in the past few days, had heard her soft crying in the night when the river was quiet.

"Patrick!" A man shouted in the distance, back toward town. Patrick unfolded his hands, caught his breath, and looked back to see a few dim lights in people's windows, candles in the dark.

"Patrick!" This time the shout was clearer, closer, and familiar. His grandfather!

"Over here!" Patrick yelled back. "I'm over here!"

Patrick tripped and fell in the darkness, picked himself up, and ran straight into the strong arms of his grandfather.

"Patrick," said the old captain, holding him tightly by the shoulders. "Where have you been? Your mother sent me out to look for you after you didn't return with your sister."

"I'm sorry. How did you know where I was?"

"The constable said he'd seen you, but that was a good while ago."

"I didn't think . . . I mean, I didn't know it had gotten to be so late."

"Didn't know?" His grandfather didn't let go of Patrick's shoulders. "How could you not? And what, pray tell, were you doing out here alone?"

"I'm sorry. Really I am." Patrick could think of nothing to say in his defense, at least nothing that didn't sound silly. "I was just worried about Pa."

"The constable told me you were looking for him."

Patrick could see his grandfather's silver beard in the darkness as they trudged quietly back together through the dark streets, back toward the safety of the paddle steamer.

"Wait." The Old Man put his hand on Patrick's shoulder before they crossed the wharf. "There's something you need to know."

Patrick froze, waiting for yet another lecture.

"I know you want to find your father." When Patrick's grandfather looked down, a light from the paddle steamer lit up the wrinkles on his face, and he ran a hand through his silver-white hair. "Sure, there's nothing I'd rather see. We all do."

"I know."

"Aye, but listen, now. We've come to a point where it's out of our hands. Do you understand what I'm telling you? You want to go crashing through the bush in the middle of the night, yelling and screaming, hoping he'll hear you and come out. But then if he did, what then?"

You sound just like Becky, thought Patrick, but he didn't dare say it out loud.

"Do you follow what I'm saying, Patrick?" The Old Man again put his hands on Patrick's shoulders, and Patrick nodded.

"Yes, sir. I know what you're saying. You're not the first one to tell me that."

"Aha, but you're not agreeing with me, would that be it?"

Patrick gulped, and his tongue felt tied in place. He couldn't . . .

At last his grandfather sighed loudly.

"Well, you're just like your father, you are. A mind of your own. I suppose that's good and all. But leastways, you'll have to promise me one thing."

"Yes, sir?"

"No more running off like this. You have your first day of school tomorrow, remember. You weren't worried about *that*, were you? Is that why you ran off?"

Patrick shook his head, but he realized afterward his grandfather probably didn't see him. When Patrick closed his eyes, he heard the sounds of the river, a dog howling, piano music from somewhere downtown. He felt his grandfather's hand on his shoulder, not a strong grip, just a touch.

"I used to be a pretty fair student, myself," said Patrick's grandfather. "Good with numbers, if you ever need any help. I'll test you now. What's twelve times twelve?"

Patrick smiled. "Thanks, Grandpa. We learned those sums a long time ago."

"Well, then, there's one other thing you'll be needing my help with before you get started with the arithmetic."

"What's that?"

"Explaining to your mother where you've been tonight."

CHAPTER 6

SCHOOLMATES

The next morning, Patrick tried to sink down almost out of sight behind a table in the back of the one-room schoolhouse. He was afraid it wasn't going to work, especially since the little girl sitting next to him kept staring at him out of the corner of her eye, the way she had since he and Becky and Michael had stepped through the door that morning. They were the new kids at Echuca School, starting school weeks after classes had begun.

The teacher, Miss Tyler, was going to call on Patrick next. Michael, standing at his table in the front of the room with the younger kids, didn't seem to mind the attention at all.

"I also have a pet koala," Michael explained. "A real live one. And I'm going to put on an animal show pretty soon, if anybody wants to come see it. My family is staying on my grandfather's paddle steamer right now, but he also lets us stay in his cabin up the river. We came back down to the *Lady Elisabeth* again to help while my grandfather fixes a few things."

"Thank you, Michael." Miss Tyler looked over her thick glasses from a neatly arranged desk at the front of the room. Her short, silver-specked hair was carefully combed and tied back, and she wore a sensible, ankle-length dark dress with black shoes that laced up over her ankles. "We appreciate knowing a little more about your family. You may sit down now."

Michael smiled and turned back to the teacher before he returned to his seat. "Oh, and one more thing. My brother, Patrick, is good friends with the prince because he met him and shook hands. We even talked!"

Patrick sank even lower as some of the children laughed out loud. *What are you talking about, Michael?* he fumed.

"Now, Patrick McWaid, will you please tell the class about your father and mother?" Miss Tyler asked when Patrick reached the front.

Patrick tried to dry his palms on his pants. In the back row, the older boy named Sebastian Weatherby was glaring at him down a long hook nose with a cross-eyed stare. The way he tapped his meaty fists together, it was a sure thing Patrick didn't want to meet up with him any time soon.

What have I ever done to him? Patrick wondered.

"Patrick?" asked the teacher.

Patrick blinked. "Well, my father is from Dublin, and my mother is from a town in Northern Ireland called Carrickfergus. Her father was a minister, you see, and they traveled around the country when she was little. That's how they met. . . ."

Patrick was warming up to the subject. He looked around the room, and everyone seemed to be listening, except for Sebastian, who was whispering something to his neighbor and ducking low under the table, right behind Patrick's seat. Miss Tyler was watching Patrick and didn't seem to notice what was going on in the rest of the class.

About ten children looked as if they were Michael's age or younger; nearly the same number were Patrick's age; and only a few, maybe five or six, were older, like Becky. Or Sebastian. The older boy kept his hand in front of his mouth, and Patrick guessed he was whispering something to the dark-haired boy sitting next to him.

"What about today?" asked the teacher. "What brings your family to Echuca? What does your father do now?"

Patrick's heart stopped as he tried desperately to think of something to say.

Don't they all know about Pa already?

"My father?" he stalled. "Uh, he was a newspaper writer back home in Dublin."

"Yes." Their teacher nodded patiently. "But I asked you about the present. Here in Echuca, what does your father do?"

"Hides in the bushes, mostly," whispered Sebastian, and Patrick heard his very English-sounding voice for the first time. Some of his friends snickered. They knew about Mr. McWaid, even if their teacher didn't.

"He's not exactly here yet," Patrick finally replied. "He has to . . . he had to . . . well, we're staying with my grandfather."

"I see." Miss Tyler still seemed puzzled, but it looked as if she would let it pass.

"Tell us about your friend the prince," teased Sebastian.

Why did Michael have to get me into this? Patrick felt his face grow warm.

"Thank you, Patrick. You may sit down. And now, class, since I know everyone is excited about the circus and the arrival of Prince Alfred, it would be a good time to read about . . ."

As the teacher went on with her history lesson, Patrick slipped back to his seat. But he jumped up when he felt something soft and squishy spreading out beneath him. Sebastian and his friends giggled, and Patrick looked down on his seat to see where someone had dumped a pile of flour-and-water white paste. It was all over his pants!

"Whatever is the matter, Patrick?" asked Miss Tyler. By that time most of the class was laughing, and Patrick's ears felt as if they were flaming.

"Who did this?" demanded Patrick, looking at the boys who sat on either side.

"Patrick?" asked their teacher, coming over to inspect the damage.

Patrick looked at Sebastian, who held up his hands innocently. When Miss Tyler finally saw what had happened, she scowled in anger, but the laughter continued.

"I will have none of this foolishness in my classroom!" she

49

shouted. Sebastian snickered behind his hand.

"Watch out, Irish boy," he whispered, and either Miss Tyler didn't hear or she didn't react. "I've got plenty more where that came from. Maybe you should just go back to Carrickfergus."

"Patrick, you may leave the schoolhouse to go clean up," Miss Tyler told him as Sebastian challenged Patrick with his eyes.

He can't do this! fumed Patrick. Before he knew what he was doing, he peeled a handful of paste from his pants and threw it down in front of Sebastian.

The paste flew up and splattered Sebastian in the face, but Patrick didn't wait to see what would happen. As fast as he could, he raced out the back of the room, flew down the stairs, and out into the street.

"Patrick!" shrieked Miss Tyler. "That was uncalled for!"

But Patrick didn't stop until he reached the *Lady Elisabeth*. He vaulted down the ladder and ran to the galley, slamming the door behind him.

Now I've really done it, he told himself as he tried to catch his breath.

A few minutes later he heard a knock on the door.

"Patrick?" asked his grandfather.

Patrick pumped more fresh water into the washbasin to rinse out the rag he had been using to clean his pants. The door creaked open.

"Back already? What happened to—"

Patrick gave the seat of his pants one more swipe and threw down the towel.

"I'm not going back there," he announced, crossing his arms. "I'm not going back to school."

"I see." His grandfather wiped his hands on a greasy rag. "Off to a good start. Don't you like the teacher?"

Patrick shrugged. "She's all right. But she's a little old, and she can't hear what the kids are whispering behind her back."

The Old Man glanced at Patrick's pants, and Patrick turned away, his face turning red.

"One of the kids in the class put paste on my seat. I didn't see it before I sat down."

"That a fact? D'you know why?"

Patrick shrugged. "I suppose I wasn't paying attention."

The Old Man chuckled. "No, I mean do you know why someone would do something like that in particular?"

"Oh." Patrick shrugged. "There's one fellow, sits behind me, I'm sure he was the one. He's English."

The Old Man nodded as if he knew what had happened. "Ah, you know how much some of those English hate us. But the same thing happened to me once when I was about your age. Not with paste, but a rotten apple, I believe it was. Somebody slipped it onto my chair. Oh, what a mess."

Patrick hadn't imagined his grandfather ever being a schoolboy.

The Old Man looked up, remembering. "Matthew Ferguson was his name. Seems to me we met out in the school yard after that, and I gave him a good lesson—or at least a good fat lip."

Patrick's grandfather put up his fists like a boxer, one in front of the other. "Here, let me show you how it's done so you can go back to the school and hold your Irish head high."

Patrick put up his hands slowly and stood before his grandfather, but he couldn't seem to make his fists move.

"Come on, boy, I said I'd show you how to defend yourself." He closed Patrick's hand into a fist. "Fingers together, now. Bend your elbows. Left hand up. Stand like this."

Patrick sighed and put down his hands. "Thanks, Grandpa, but . . ."

"What's wrong with you, lad?"

"Nothing. Suppose I just don't want to hit anybody."

The Old Man looked at his grandson more carefully, as if he had never seen him before.

"Well, I wanted to hit him when I threw the paste," Patrick admitted. "I get so mad sometimes."

The Old Man grinned, but it didn't make Patrick feel any better.

"But then it goes away," continued Patrick, and his grandfather slowly lowered his fists.

"Yet your good Irish name doesn't go away, now, does it, boy?"

Patrick frowned, wondering about what his grandfather had said.

"Forgive me another sermon, lad, and this from a man who doesn't darken the door of a church more than thrice a year, but you have to see it's as plain as the nose on your face."

The Old Man took a deep breath. "You've got to use your fists. You've got to fight your way through life." He tried poking at Patrick with a couple of gentle jabs, but Patrick only put up his palms in defense, and the Old Man sighed. "Of course, I suppose that's not what your mother or your Bible would say, now, is it?"

Patrick didn't answer. He didn't want to argue with his grandfather, but he knew what his father had always told him about watching his temper, about never hitting back.

"All right," his grandfather finally sighed. "I can't say I understand you. But if you change your mind, I'll be glad to teach you a thing or two."

Patrick looked at his hands again, and the Old Man paused by the door before he left.

"Ah, you're surely just like your father. He had quite a temper when he was a lad, just like you. But for some reason I could never teach him to fight, either."

On his way out of the boat, Grandpa nearly ran into Patrick's mother, who was coming in with an armload of supplies.

"Oh!" she said, noticing Patrick as she put down the groceries on a counter. "What is going on here? Aren't Becky and Michael in school?"

"They are, Sarah." The Old Man stepped up and put his arm around Patrick to lead him out of the room. "Patrick just had to tend to some business here. He's on his way back to class, aren't you, now, Patrick?"

Patrick hesitated for a moment as his grandfather towed him out the door.

"Sure, yes. I suppose."

"You *suppose*? And what should I understand that to mean, boy?" The Old Man didn't wait for an answer as they stepped out on deck. "Your pants look fine now. You just go on back there and take your place. Remember, McWaids are fighters. All of them."

Patrick sighed as he climbed the ladder back to the wharf.

Maybe Sebastian and Grandpa would like to go a few rounds, he thought, and the idea of his grandfather boxing with a schoolboy seemed almost funny.

"Hurry back to school, now!" the Old Man called after him, and Patrick started to trot back down the street.

What else can I do? he asked himself, remembering what he had said about never going back.

To save time, he cut through an alley behind Mullarky's General Store, a dirt trail between two rows of buildings that Mr. Mullarky probably used for his supply wagons. One was parked in back of the store, a single horse still harnessed and a load of canvas piled high in the back. As Patrick turned the corner, a man in the driver's seat jumped down and into the store.

"Need some more rope, quickly!" the man yelled at someone Patrick couldn't see. Patrick recognized him as one of the circus people, one of the men who had come for the elephants last night, when they had been turned loose in the river.

Wonder what's the big hurry? thought Patrick, slowing to a walk. He heard a groan from the back of the wagon, and Patrick froze when he saw something move under the canvas.

Is someone in there? he wondered, but the shape looked too big. The creature under the canvas wiggled again, and Patrick was sure it was an animal of some kind.

It's just so big. It can only be . . .

Slowly, carefully, he pulled up a corner of the canvas. Underneath he saw a tangle of net, and then something furry and orange whipped out and hit him squarely in the face.

"Oh!" he cried, jumping back and throwing the canvas back down. "A tiger tail!"

The creature—or the tiger—growled again as the wagon driver burst through the back door into the alley, a huge coil of heavy rope slung over his shoulder.

"Hey, kid!" he yelled. "Get away from that wagon!"

Patrick was glad to obey, racing as fast as he could away from the man and the tiger, back to school. Even Sebastian was better than a tiger!

CHAPTER 7

THE FIGHT

As he neared the school, Patrick figured it had to be recess, since some of the students were out in the dirt yard behind the school, running races. But the teacher was nowhere in sight, and neither was Michael nor his sister.

"Hey, Irish boy!" Sebastian Weatherby popped out from behind a tree. "I've been waiting for you."

"Sorry to keep you waiting." Patrick tried to get past the older boy, but Sebastian stepped in front of him. Several of the bully's friends stepped behind the two of them.

"What do you want?" asked Patrick. After being surprised by a tiger, Sebastian was a bit of a letdown. Patrick felt more annoyed than anything else.

"Just wanted to make sure you were all right."

The other boys laughed. Patrick just stared straight ahead.

"Why are you bothering me? I don't even know you."

"And that's the way we're going to keep it." Sebastian rubbed his nose and checked around the small school yard. Still no Miss Tyler. "But I just wanted you to know that we have a special initiation for Irish kids who come to this school."

Patrick tried to walk by once more, but the other boy stopped him with a shove.

"Did I say you could leave yet?"

"I don't need your permission."

"Ohh." Sebastian looked at his friends with a smirk. "Here's a tough one."

Sebastian slammed his heavy foot down on Patrick's toes, hard, so Patrick couldn't move.

"But you know what, Irish boy?" Sebastian smiled. "I'm going to give you an advantage, just this first time. I'm going to let you take the first punch, since you'll never be able to touch me again."

Sebastian made a show of sticking out his chin and pointing at it. He even closed his eyes.

"Come on, little Irish boy. This is your first and last chance."

Patrick yanked his foot free and tried to push past the other boy, but Sebastian's friends held him back.

"Look, I don't know what your problem is," said Patrick, "but I am not going to fight you. Fight yourself."

By that time many of the other kids had gathered around, waiting for the fight to begin.

"Hit him, Patrick," urged one boy. "It's the only chance you'll ever get!"

The shouts reminded him of his grandfather's words: *"Remember, Patrick, McWaids are fighters."*

Not this McWaid, Patrick decided, crossing his arms stubbornly. *Not this kind of fighting.*

Patrick glared at Sebastian. The other boys wouldn't let him escape.

"Well?" asked Sebastian, opening his eyes. "I'm getting impatient. It looks as if I may have to teach you a lesson."

Patrick felt himself shoved from behind, and he stumbled right into Sebastian, who fell backward.

"You little wombat!" cried Sebastian, turning to the crowd. His face was red. "You saw him push me down. He started this!"

Patrick tried to pick himself up, but with the speed of a snake striking its victim, Sebastian was on him with a vicious swing that connected squarely with Patrick's jaw. Patrick felt his teeth snap together with a horrible click and collapsed into the arms of the boys who had shoved him. They picked him up and pushed him right back.

"Hit him!" cried another boy, and the rest of the crowd started up a cheer. Patrick couldn't tell whom they were cheering for. He rubbed his chin and studied his opponent, wondering where his usual temper had disappeared to.

"Come on," yelled someone else, "before Miss Tyler gets here."

Patrick imagined the stance his grandfather had been trying to teach him. Left fist up, right fist back by his shoulder, feet spread apart. But he didn't put his hands up—or couldn't. Instead, he just stood there, waiting for the next blow.

"You know," Patrick heard himself saying, "I guess I feel sorry for you."

Sebastian laughed. *"You* feel sorry for *me*? That's hard to believe."

Sebastian connected again, this time glancing off Patrick's cheekbone and eye before Patrick could duck. He fell to his knees just as he heard a handbell ring.

"Boys!" Miss Tyler shouted. "Boys! Stop this at once!"

As soon as the crowd parted to let her in, Sebastian grabbed his stomach, groaned, and started rolling in the dust.

"Ohh," he almost sobbed in pretend pain. "The new boy hit me in the stomach. Ohh!"

The acting was so good Patrick almost believed he had actually hit the other boy, and the teacher bent down to see what had happened to Sebastian.

"What happened here?" She looked up at the other boys who had crowded around.

"He came running at Sebastian and said he was going to get him," said a smaller, dark-haired boy whose name Patrick couldn't remember.

"Ohh," Sebastian added another groan for effect. "I think he might have broken my rib."

"Oh, come on." Patrick sighed, and his own eye throbbed with pain. "I didn't hit anyone. He's the one—"

Miss Tyler helped the moaning Sebastian to his feet, and he

gripped his side as if he were in pain.

"You come and lie down, Sebastian," said Miss Tyler, holding him around the shoulders. She shot a sharp glance at Patrick. "And *you* follow us, young man. I'm going to have to speak to your parents about this incident. We may have to decide if you'll be allowed to continue classes here. Honestly, on the very first day you're here!"

"But everyone saw what really happened. . . ." began Patrick. He sighed, already sure it was no use. Sebastian glanced back at him with a sneer while his three friends walked behind Patrick, kicking his heels.

I wonder if Pa ever felt like this, he thought as they paraded back into the schoolhouse.

Michael met them at the door, smiling and waving a book. "I finished the assignment, Miss . . ." His voice dropped off, and his eyes grew wide when he saw their group.

"Excuse us, Michael," interrupted Miss Tyler. "But could you please lay out the cot in the corner for Sebastian? He's been injured."

Sebastian groaned again, loudly enough for everyone in the room to hear. Miss Tyler nearly ran into Becky, who had the same expression on her face as her little brother.

"Becky, no one will listen to me," Patrick explained to his sister. "I didn't even touch him."

Becky looked over at Sebastian, who gasped for air as he leaned against a table, his head bowed. That's when Patrick rediscovered the temper he thought had left him.

"Stand up, you big actor!"

Before he even thought about what he was doing, Patrick grabbed Sebastian by the arm and hauled him up straight. "Go on, tell them how you hit me. You're not hurt. Tell Miss Tyler."

"Patrick!" Miss Tyler stood in between the two boys and removed Patrick's hand from Sebastian's shirt collar. "You'll not start the fight again right here in the schoolroom!"

"I'm not, Miss Tyler, I was just—"

"No." She interrupted him. "I've seen enough. You will leave immediately, and I don't want to see you back here again unless you come with your parents and a full apology!"

Patrick stared at the teacher, and his mouth dropped open.

"Do I make myself clear, young man?"

Patrick could only nod, while Sebastian flashed him a quick smirk from behind Miss Tyler's back.

Becky looked at her brother helplessly.

"I'll be fine, Becky," he said, turning around without another word.

Patrick stumbled down the four steps of the schoolhouse, bumped into the water pump, and hurried his step. He touched his tender right eye and winced.

First the paste, now this, he thought. By then he noticed that his entire right eye had swollen shut. *I suppose it can't get any worse.*

Then he thought about what his mother would say when he got back to the *Lady Elisabeth*. And he caught sight of the Old Man walking down the street in his direction.

Or maybe it can get worse.

Patrick's grandfather was balancing a small wooden barrel on his shoulder, whistling as he walked. Patrick tried to duck out of sight, but it was too late.

"Hey, Patrick!" yelled his grandfather. "Hold up, there."

Patrick tried to stand sideways, with his black eye facing away from his grandfather, and he scratched his forehead with his left hand, shielding the eye.

"Don't tell me you've not been back to school yet?"

"Uh, yes, sir, I've been back."

The Old Man shifted the weight of his barrel. "What, then? Did you run out?"

"In a way." Patrick continued scratching his forehead, and his grandfather leaned closer for a better look.

"Something wrong?" he asked. He pulled Patrick's hand gently away, then turned Patrick to face him.

"Well, now!" beamed the Old Man. "Why didn't you say you got in a fight? That's quite a shiner."

Patrick nodded. It still hurt.

"I knew you'd take my advice." The Old Man grinned from ear to ear and boxed the air with one hand. "So how did you do with the other fellow? Make any good hits?"

Patrick frowned and turned away. "I didn't hit him, Grandpa."

The Old Man stopped his boxing. "Not at all? Not even a—"

"I didn't even fight him. He just came up to me and started hitting."

"Why . . ." The Old Man's mood changed like a storm cloud. "That's not a fair fight. But you didn't even put up your fists and fight like a McWaid?"

Patrick shook his head.

"Explain it to your mother, then. She's just coming out of that store."

Patrick looked through the nearby store window to see his mother rushing out.

"Patrick!" she cried, rushing up to him. She took his chin in her hand. "Whatever happened?"

"Ma," he protested, pulling his head back. "Not here. It's nothing."

"Nothing?" she replied. "You meet me on the street with a horrible black eye on your first day of school, and you say it's nothing? What is going on? You can't even see out of that eye, it's so swollen."

"No need to get upset, Sarah." The Old Man stepped up. "The boy was in a fight, that's all. And from the look of it, he took most of the blows."

"Yes, and maybe they used Patrick for a punching bag. Patrick?"

"Ah, leave him alone. He'll be fine once he learns how to defend himself like a man."

But Mrs. McWaid wasn't listening. "You march straight down to the boat, Patrick McWaid, and wait for me. I'll be there in a minute, and you're going to tell me everything that happened."

CHAPTER 8

APOLOGY

The next morning, Friday, Patrick slowly dragged his way back up Pakenham Street to the public school. He still wasn't sure what he was going to say when Miss Tyler demanded his apology.

"Come on, Patrick," his mother told him as Becky and Michael ran ahead. Miss Tyler stood on the front steps of her building, ringing her bell.

"Mrs. McWaid?" The teacher pulled Patrick's mother aside while Patrick stood waiting.

"Go on inside, Patrick," Miss Tyler told him with a nod.

Patrick sighed with relief as the door slammed behind him, until Sebastian bumped into him from the side and yanked Patrick's book out of his hand. It clattered to the floor.

Sebastian chuckled. "Sorry about that. I wouldn't want you to get in trouble again, even before you get back."

"Pick it up, please," Patrick ordered quietly. He had forgotten that Sebastian was several inches taller and weighed at least twenty pounds more than he did, but just then it didn't seem to matter. All Patrick could see was Sebastian with his chin stuck out at him, his lips peeled back to show a full set of crooked teeth.

"Oh, so now you want both eyes to match, is that it?" Sebastian snickered and stepped on the corner of the book with a muddy shoe.

Patrick bent down to pick up the book, but Sebastian kept his foot planted firmly on the corner. Everything was quiet except for the words ringing in Patrick's ears.

"McWaids are fighters," he heard his grandfather telling him. *"McWaids are fighters."*

For a second Patrick was ready to tackle the bigger boy, but his sister spoke up.

"Patrick, don't," Becky warned him.

Sebastian grinned. "Better listen to your sister, Irish boy."

Patrick squinted at the older boy and saw a glimmer of fear in his eyes—something he hadn't seen before.

"So why didn't *your* parents have to come to school this morning?" asked Patrick.

Sebastian squinted at him. "Don't have any parents," he snapped.

"I'm sorry," Patrick started to whisper, but just then Miss Tyler stepped in, and the rest of the class rose to their feet.

A pig-tailed girl in the front row was the first to raise her hand after everyone had sat down. It looked urgent.

"Yes, Edwina?" Miss Tyler had already opened their ciphering book, the first class of the day before catechism, grammar, writing, and geography.

"The new boy was going to hit Sebastian. He was red in the face."

"Is that right?" Miss Tyler arched her eyebrows in surprise.

Patrick looked down at the table where he sat with three other students, all of them a few years younger. He wished his friend Jack Duggan were there instead of having to help his father at the boatyard that week.

"Is that correct, Patrick?" He could already hear the leather strap in her hand. "You know that I will not tolerate any more of this foolishness in my classroom."

"No, ma'am," he answered back. "We weren't fighting."

"But almost fighting?"

"He stepped on my book, ma'am."

"I tried to tell him it was an accident," Sebastian piped up, sounding very sorry for himself.

"I don't believe it was," countered Patrick.

The room was silent except for the ticking of the wall clock behind Miss Tyler's desk. It hung right next to the small, fly-specked portrait of a scowling Queen Victoria.

Finally their teacher cleared her throat. "Because you are new to this class, I shall not be administering corporal punishment, though it is against my better judgment."

Patrick sighed in relief.

"But I will not tolerate any more impertinence from you, Patrick McWaid, nor from you, Sebastian Weatherby, and I will not hesitate to use this strap if necessary. Do I make myself understood?"

"Yes, ma'am." Patrick still didn't look up.

Sebastian mumbled something that sounded like "I understand."

"Very well. Now, Patrick, I want you to stand and apologize to Sebastian for your part in the incident yesterday, and after that Sebastian shall do likewise. Patrick?"

Patrick stood and cleared his throat, trying to think of what to say.

"Stand and face him, please."

Patrick turned around.

"Better make it good," whispered one of Sebastian's friends. Someone giggled, but Miss Tyler didn't hear.

"I'm sorry . . ." Patrick finally managed. "And I don't hold it against you that you're English."

The class laughed while Miss Tyler banged her ruler against her desk.

"That's enough, class. Sebastian? Your turn."

Sebastian still had his arms crossed. "I apologize, too. I don't know what for, but I apologize, I suppose."

"That sounded less than genuine, boys, but go ahead and shake hands now."

Patrick squinted and stuck out his hand.

Sebastian grinned. "No hard feelings, Irish boy. You can't help who your parents are any more than I can."

Patrick wasn't sure what to make of the other boy's apology, but when he sat down and looked in the palm of his hand he discovered a chewed-up wad of paper. Someone giggled again behind him.

"Very well." Miss Tyler finally smiled, but stiffly. "We start today with ciphering. Please open your *Bartlett's Exercise Book* and follow along on page fourteen: 'If eight men, six women, and twelve boys do a job in twenty-four days of nine hours, in how many days of eight hours will twelve men, fifteen women, and ten boys do three times as much work, supposing two women do as much as five boys and one man as much as two women?' "

Patrick got rid of the spit wad, closed his eyes, and buried his face in his arithmetic book, what Miss Tyler called "ciphering."

I wonder if Grandpa knows how to do this kind of question.

He had a headache, and it wasn't even nine-thirty.

The headache lasted until three in the afternoon, when Miss Tyler stood by the door and watched her students file out for the day. She stopped Patrick and motioned for him to wait.

"I know you're a bright boy," she told him after everyone had left. It seemed like the first kind thing she had said to him all day. He nodded without replying, wondering what she meant.

"No one else got the correct answer to the ciphering problem, not even your sister."

Patrick grinned. He couldn't help it.

"But you're certainly not off to a good start, what with your fighting. And you can't be making friends here with all your tall tales about being captured by bushrangers and that time you say you jumped into the sea to rescue an American sailor. . . ."

"I only answered what others asked me."

"Yes, quite. And your brother boasting about your personal meeting with Prince Alfred. Surely you know it sounds as if you're spinning a lot of tall tales."

"Michael makes it sound larger than life, Miss Tyler." Patrick sighed, but what else could he say?

She raised her eyebrows.

"And Sebastian did step on my book on purpose."

Miss Tyler frowned and nodded. At least Sebastian had finally stopped pestering him. In fact, he hadn't heard a word from the boy or his friends the rest of the day.

"Oh, and Patrick?"

"Yes, Miss Tyler?"

"Please avoid any terrible accidents or adventures between now and Monday, will you?"

"I'll try, Miss Tyler."

CHAPTER 9

THE CLOWN'S SECRET

"What a sight," said Mrs. McWaid that evening as she looked around at the crowd that had packed the circus tent. "Will you look at all these people?"

Prince Alfred, duke of Edinburgh, was back in town; he had a special section set up for him, decorated with bright red, blue, and white Union Jacks—the flag of Great Britain—and what seemed like miles of bunting. Patrick and his family had managed to squeeze into one of the top rows, all the way on the other side of the prince.

"Look, there's one of the horses we saw swimming in the river!" Michael pointed at a trio of horses that had started to gallop in circles in the middle of the main ring. He bounced with excitement as a woman in a sparkling blue outfit stood upright on one of the glistening white animals, waving her arms for balance.

But still no tiger, thought Patrick, fidgeting on the hard wooden bench.

"Aren't you excited, Patrick?" asked Michael, his face beaming.

Patrick nodded but turned his head to listen for the growls and snarls he had heard before when the circus had first come to town. All he could hear was the brass band, the applause of the crowd, and the whip snaps of the circus ringleader. In between, he could hear raindrops on the roof and side of the tent, too.

"How's your eye, Patrick?" asked his sister, leaning over in her seat. She winced when she looked at Patrick's face.

"It's fine now." Patrick reached up to check his black eye. "Ow!"

"It just looks so horrible," replied Becky. "All puffy and black. Can you even see out of it?"

"I can see out of it fine. Anyway, it's a lot better than it was before."

"And now, Your Highness, ladies, and gentlemen, if you would direct your attention . . ." A man with tall, dark riding boots and a matching black hat stood in the center of it all, and his voice seemed to vibrate the striped tent walls. Michael looked hypnotized, following his every move down on the sawdust floor.

"Hey, Patrick," yelled someone from several seats over. "Talked to your friend the prince yet?"

Patrick groaned when he saw Sebastian sitting next to three of his friends from school. The other boys laughed and clapped, but it wasn't at the circus act.

"Someone you know from school?" asked Mrs. McWaid.

"That's the boy who put the paste on Patrick's chair," announced Michael. "And the one who punched him in the eye."

"Oh, is *that* the boy?" Their mother frowned. "Well, don't look at him."

"Just ignore them, Patrick," agreed Becky, watching the clowns bumping into each other. "That way, they won't bother you as much."

Michael wrinkled his nose at the boys, while Patrick pretended to watch the show.

"I'll be right back," Patrick whispered into his sister's ear. He dropped over the back edge of the low platform they were all sitting on. He hoped Sebastian and his friends didn't notice.

"Patrick?" His mother checked on him.

But he just waved back and repeated to her what he had already told Becky, adding, "I'm fine, Ma."

By that time everyone in the tent—and that included half the town of Echuca—was concentrating on the riding act. It looked like the acrobats were next; they were standing outside an open tent flap, trotting in place and stretching in their matching green tights, trying to stay out of the rain. Patrick moved quietly between two of the acrobats, then turned and slipped under a rope between two tents.

A huge draft horse tied outside the tent kicked backward, but Patrick was quick enough to jump clear. He stood for a moment between a couple of wagons, back where the circus people had parked most of their gear. They would be in Echuca only a few days, but several of the performers had their own tents. There were pens for the animals under the trees, including the three elephants. He would have gone over to see them, but some men were there, and he was looking for something else. He stopped a clown who was hurrying past.

Might as well ask, thought Patrick. "Excuse me, I'm looking for the tigers."

The clown stared at Patrick as if he were speaking another language.

"The tigers?" repeated Patrick, a little more slowly. "Don't you have three tigers, the way it said on your posters?"

The clown's white makeup started to run down his collar. He shook his head.

"No, no tigers here. Go back to the show now. You shouldn't be back here."

That's what I thought he'd say, thought Patrick. He nodded and thanked the man but waited to see where he went. Sure enough, the clown hurried away and stepped into another tent. An irritated voice boomed out into the rainy evening.

"Not *another* kid asking about the tigers?"

The clown answered something Patrick couldn't understand, and the irritated man interrupted.

"What do I have to do, go out there myself and track down all of them?"

More whimpering from the clown.

"And *I'm* telling you that finding one isn't good enough. Those cats cost us a lot of money, and our audiences are going to start asking questions if they don't see them performing. Understand?"

Even though he could make out only one side of the conversation, Patrick was pretty sure he knew what was going on.

"All right, fine, but now your act is over. I don't want to see you again until you're back with the animals, got it? We've got plenty of nets, and I just bought some more ropes. Only don't use the gun."

When Patrick got up enough courage to peek around the side of the tent, he came almost face-to-face with the clown.

"You again?" Only the man's makeup was smiling. "Am I going to have to call your parents to come get you? The show's in there, like I told you before." The clown pointed back at the tent with his thumb, and Patrick lowered his head and reluctantly shuffled back. But just before he crossed the rope again, he spied a large box, large enough to pack a small elephant inside. It was draped securely with tarps.

Patrick looked around, then tiptoed quickly over to take a look. He had to find out for himself.

If the cats are really out there, Pa is in danger.

He pulled the canvas back gingerly, half expecting to hear a roar or see a powerful paw slash out at him.

It's a cage, all right.

He gripped one of the iron bars and crouched down to see what was inside. In the corner, a tiger snarled at him. The animal's leg was bandaged, though, and he didn't move but hissed, showing a large set of sharp white teeth. Even though the tiger wasn't going anywhere, Patrick quickly backed away.

This has to be the same tiger I saw in the wagon, he thought, stepping back carefully. He noticed a plaque on the bottom of the cage.

" '*Felis tigris,*' " he read out loud, and a voice from behind made him jump.

"I thought I told you to get back to the show," barked the clown. "Out!"

"Sorry. I'm on my way."

This time, though, Patrick was determined to find out more.

"What happened to the other two tigers?" he asked. From what he had overheard, Patrick was pretty sure he already knew.

The clown didn't answer right away, only pulled the canvas back down over the cage and grabbed Patrick's shirt collar.

"There's only one tiger in that cage, boy. And he's sick, so he's not in the show."

"But what about the roars we heard the night you came to town? You—"

"As I told you," replied the clown, shoving Patrick roughly back under the rope barrier, "we have only one tiger."

"But your posters in town say—"

"No tigers, understand? That was a misprint. No tigers. Not here, not anywhere. Now, *get out* and stay out. I don't want to see you back here again!"

Patrick took one last look at the covered cage before he retreated back inside the main tent. The horses were finished with their tricks; now two acrobats were balancing on stacked-up chairs. He could see his mother's face in the crowd, looking his way, and he waved.

"What took you so long, Patrick?" His sister stepped up beside him, and she brushed her hair away from her eyes. "Ma sent me out to find you."

Patrick pulled her to the edge of the tent.

"I heard some of the circus people talking out there," he told her.

The crowd cheered and Becky shook her head. "What? I can't hear you."

"I said, the circus people are looking for the missing tigers, but they can't find them. I saw one, but I know there are at least two tigers loose out there!"

A woman walking with her little girl turned to look at them with wide eyes.

"Worst thing is," he continued, "if Pa's still out there, well, then . . ."

He didn't have to explain.

CHAPTER 10

MURRAY RIVER GUNBOAT

"Look at me!" Michael tried to do a handstand on the deck of the *Lady Elisabeth*, but it was wet and his hand slipped out from under him.

"Don't hurt yourself, Michael," Becky warned him.

He rubbed his chin and squinted up at the blustery Saturday morning sky. After the circus had let out, they had stayed overnight on their grandfather's paddle steamer again, closer to town.

"I'm not going to hurt myself. I'm practicing for 'Michael McWaid and His Wild Animal Show.'"

"How can you think about that kind of thing right now?" Becky asked.

But Patrick couldn't help chuckling. "I can just see it now: 'Magnificent Michael McWaid and his amazing pet koala, Christopher! Watch Christopher eat leaves. Watch Christopher sleep. Bring your own pillow and take a nap, it's so boring! Watch—'"

"You're not any fun, Patrick," protested Michael, holding up his sleepy little koala. "Watch, Christopher is going to show you how he can swing."

Michael had attached the ends of a couple of strong cords to the railing on the upper deck, making a swing for his pet.

"You're not really going to put that animal on that swing, are you?" asked Becky.

"Why not?" Michael wanted to know.

"Indeed, what if the little creature falls off?" asked their grandfather, leaning over the upper railing.

"Oh, Captain," Michael smiled up at their grandfather, "we didn't know you were up already."

"With all the noise you children were making, how could I not be?"

The Old Man climbed down the ladder to join them, then carefully lifted Christopher the koala from his swing.

"I'm afraid Becky and Patrick were right," he said. "This is no swing for a wee koala."

Michael frowned.

"But I have a finer idea for your show," continued the Old Man, settling down on his hands and knees. "We'll have a daring horse and rider act."

"Are you sure?" Michael smiled, not quite knowing what to make of the stern paddle-steamer captain playing horse with them.

"Better climb aboard before I change my mind!" boomed the Old Man, rearing up on his legs and pawing at the air with his hands. "This is one wild horse."

Becky laughed and clapped her hands as the Old Man added a whole stable full of horse sounds to his act. Michael and his koala struggled to hang on.

"Tip him over, Grandpa!" shouted Patrick.

"Ah, my poor bruised knees," protested the Old Man. "I didn't realize you were going to be so heavy, my boy. What have you been eating?"

They collapsed, laughing, when Patrick heard another noise directly above them.

"Easy, now!" someone shouted from the wharf. They heard the grinding of a steam-driven crane, the kind men used to load and unload paddle steamers on the wharf. Patrick looked up to see Prince Alfred's aide, still gripping his black leather notebook.

"You, below," cried the man. "Out of the way, if you please!"

As Patrick and his sister stood staring, the small crane's pulley began lowering a miniature cannon toward the rear deck of the

Lady Elisabeth. Their grandfather rolled over on his back and stared up in amazement.

"Does he know about this?" asked Becky.

Patrick shrugged. "I never heard him say anything about a cannon. It's kind of cute, though. Just our size."

"Perfect for the Michael McWaid Wild Animal Show," said Michael. "Now we can shoot flying kangaroos out of the cannon."

Patrick smiled. "Maybe we can shoot *you*."

The Old Man got to his feet, put his hands on his hips, and looked with surprise at the man directing the operation.

"You'll kindly tell me what would be happening here?" he asked, stepping directly underneath the cannon and crossing his arms. "I wasn't told anything about a cannon."

The crane screeched to a stop, and the man with the notebook leaned out over the edge of the wharf.

"Look, mister, ah—"

"Captain. I'm the captain of this vessel. And you are?"

"Wilkinson, my dear Captain. Aide, bodyguard, and personal secretary to His Royal Highness Prince Alfred, duke of Edinburgh."

"Sure, and I suppose you tell everyone that."

Wilkinson didn't smile at the Old Man's dry humor, only pulled out a handkerchief from his vest pocket, rubbed his forehead thoroughly, refolded the handkerchief, and carefully replaced it, with a proper point showing.

"Yes, well, Captain, as you can see, we've taken the trouble to rise quite early this morning, and now we're merely lowering this cannon into place as we arranged earlier."

"If that's so," replied the Old Man in his unmistakable Irish brogue, "then I'd like to know who's been doing all the arranging. Because it surely didn't include me."

By this time the aide was busy leafing through his notebook, mumbling the whole time. The two dock workers handling the crane looked nervously from one man to the other, waiting for instructions.

"Yes, yes, here it is." The aide stabbed at a page in his notebook, then held it out as if everyone could read it from twenty feet away.

"It says right here that we should be loading the ceremonial cannon on the rear deck of the *Viola* no later than six-forty-five on the morning of Saturday, June 6, 1868."

The Old Man scratched his chin through his silver beard. He didn't budge from his position directly under the swinging cannon.

"You got the time right," he began slowly. "The date and the year, too."

"Well, then?" The aide slammed his notebook shut as if the matter were settled.

"But you'll find the *Viola* over there." The Old Man chuckled. "And somehow I doubt you'll be going anywhere on her just now."

They all looked at where the Old Man was pointing, toward the Belson's Red Gum Works and Boatyard, where a good number of Murray River paddle steamers were launched or repaired. The *Viola*, it seemed, was taking a long-needed rest on the bank and stood sagging and tilted on the shore.

"That's the vessel we were to have take the prince on his daytrip?" Wilkinson checked his notebook once again. "It's full of holes!"

"Up for repairs last week." The Old Man studied the cannon waving in the breeze.

"Oh dear, oh dear." Wilkinson scribbled some notes in his book and looked up and down the river. "His Majesty was set on visiting your . . . whatever is the name of your eucalyptus forest nearby?"

"Barmah," replied Michael. "The Barmah Forest."

"Exactly. But now we must find a replacement vessel to charter."

"I wish you luck." The Old Man wiped his hands. "But I must insist now that you take your cannon back."

"Why doesn't the prince ride the *Lady E*?" asked Michael.

"Hush, Michael," said the Old Man.

Before Michael could say anything else, the prince's covered carriage pulled up to the edge of the wharf. Unannounced, the right door flew open before Wilkinson could grab the handle.

"Ah, Wilkinson," said the prince, stepping out into the sun as if he himself were shot out of the cannon. "I see you have arrangements already in order for our trip."

The prince frowned only a moment when he noticed the crane and the cannon. "And for the installation of your ceremonial cannon. You do know that I'd prefer not to bring it, but if you insist . . ."

"Yes, of course, Your Highness," stuttered Wilkinson. "But it's all arranged. We were just placing it on the deck, weren't we, Captain?"

The Old Man looked up at the prince and tugged at his beard.

"Beggin' your pardon, sir, but this is a regular cargo vessel, and a small one at that, with but two staterooms and not a lot of fancy accommodations. I have some supplies I'll have to be running up to Yarrawonga. There might not be—"

"Splendid!" interrupted the prince. "I'm quite interested in seeing the river firsthand, so I've instructed Wilkinson to charter a typical Murray River steamboat. I see he hasn't failed me, Captain. We'll be ready to sail this morning, then?"

"Precisely at eleven," pronounced Wilkinson, patting his notebook.

The Old Man's silver eyebrows knit a little closer, but finally the captain of the *Lady Elisabeth* nodded. "We'll be ready. Let's just hope it doesn't start pouring rain again. It's hardly let up."

Wilkinson sighed with relief and consulted his notebook once more. "Very well, then, flags, bunting, and other decorations should be delivered here to the wharf within the quarter hour."

"Can we help decorate?" asked Michael.

The Old Man frowned and returned to his wheelhouse while Wilkinson licked his lips and pointed at the crane operators.

"Very well, now, boys, what are you waiting for? Lower it to the deck."

Patrick glanced up at the operators, who had stood back while the men were talking. He heard the gears click threateningly, then saw Michael following his grandfather right under the heavy, teetering cannon. "Michael!" he shouted. Patrick knew he had only an instant before the cannon would drop straight onto Michael's head.

CHAPTER 11

POST OFFICE CLUE

Becky told them later that the two men on the crane had lunged at the crank handle to keep it from slipping. She could tell they did all they could to keep the heavy iron cannon from crushing Michael.

Even Hugh Wilkinson, the prince's aide, would have his own stories about how time seemed to stand still for that one horrible moment after the cannon slipped loose.

Patrick didn't know any of that at the time. All he could see was Michael strolling happily across the deck, right in the path of a ton of falling metal.

"Michael!" cried Patrick as he launched himself at his brother. He tackled him around the waist and threw him to the deck.

I'm going to wake up dead under a cannon, Patrick thought as they hit hard and rolled. Forgetting the pain in his black eye, he closed his eyes to the sound of shouting and wood splintering. Then everything was quiet.

"Why did you do that, Patrick?" Michael sounded far away as he tried to scramble clear.

Patrick opened his eyes.

"Patrick!" His grandfather sounded anxious. "Are you all right?"

"Dear me! Is he hurt?" called the prince.

Good question, thought Patrick. He tried wiggling his toes on both feet, then looked around to see what had happened.

The top half of the little cannon had partially crushed the paddle steamer's wooden deck, but it hadn't crashed all the way through. Another few inches, and it might have taken his foot through a gaping hole in the deck.

"I'm fine," announced Michael. "Except for Patrick smothering me."

"Better than ending up underneath that."

"Oh." Michael saw the hole for the first time. His eyes widened as he looked at the cannon, then at Patrick sitting on the deck, then back at the cannon.

"You're really all right, lads?" The Old Man hoisted Michael into his arms. "And now what'll be done about *this*, Mr. Wilkinson?" His face grew crimson red as he stood next to the cannon.

The prince's aide licked his lips and swallowed hard.

"As long as we're all unhurt," said the prince, stepping between the men, "I suggest we make temporary repairs before departing. Naturally, we shall reimburse you completely, Captain, for your expenses, just as we surely would if anything else were to happen to your vessel. Write that down, Wilkinson."

The Old Man looked as if he might have said something else, but a wagon piled high with wooden crates arrived at the wharf.

"Flags and bunting?" asked the driver, a boy in his late teens. He took one look at the cannon wedged into the deck and raised an eyebrow. "Am I in the right place?"

"Right on time," replied Wilkinson, checking off something in his book. "Perhaps we can get this little ship looking proper yet."

"*Proper?*" sputtered the Old Man. "You've done a fine job of it thus far!"

Wilkinson ignored the protest and continued his directions. "Now, if you children will help, we'll unload these crates and decorate this vessel."

The Old Man put Michael down, patted him on the shoulder, and disappeared up the ladder to his wheelhouse without another word.

"Don't worry about my grandpa," Michael whispered to the prince. "He's really nice when you get to know him."

"I'm sure he is." Prince Alfred smiled. "So is Mr. Wilkinson, though he's overly concerned with appearances, as you probably gather."

"Here you go." Wilkinson didn't seem to hear what anyone said about him; he just started handing down crates filled with bunting and Union Jacks while the two men with the crane hoisted the cannon slowly back up. One of the workers nailed a few stout boards over the hole in the deck, and the cannon was fitted to a spot in the middle of the rear deck, facing back.

"Where do we put these flags?" Patrick asked his sister, who was holding one end of a long red streamer.

"Hang them from all the higher places"—she pointed—"like along the top deck."

Patrick took a hammer, some tacks, and three flags with him up to the top deck, where the Old Man was trying to stay out of their way.

"Careful of those tacks," grunted the Old Man. "You want to be able to pull them out again."

"Yes, sir." Patrick nodded as he brought the hammer squarely down on his thumb. "Ohh!" He gripped his finger and hunched over, dropping his flag to the deck below.

"Oh, Patrick." The Old Man dropped to his knees next to his grandson. "You're aiming for the nail, not the finger, aren't you, now?"

Patrick couldn't say anything as his finger throbbed with pain.

"I'm afraid the accidents are catching up with you, lad. First the black eye, and now . . ." The Old Man stood by Patrick for few moments, and neither of them spoke until the prince's aide came marching in quickstep across the deck, his heels clicking.

"Ah, there's that popinjay Wilkinson," muttered the Old Man, shaking his head. "He's going to have so many flags on the old *Lady E*, we won't be able to see out to steer up the river." Patrick's grandfather turned to face him again.

"Listen, lad, you've done enough around here for now. Why

don't you run up to Mullarky's for me before it starts raining again. I believe there are a couple of crates of supplies we've yet to pick up."

"More food?" asked Michael.

The Old Man nodded. "Something like that. Think you can do it, now, without running into trouble?"

"Or Sebastian?" added Michael.

Patrick nodded. "Sure, I can. Come on, Michael."

"I'm going, too," said Becky.

Michael bounded along behind his brother and sister, pretending he was a lion or a lion tamer, Patrick wasn't sure which. Just to be sure, Patrick looked three times before crossing Warren Street. He stopped when they reached Echuca's small brick post office.

"Say, can you two get the supplies?" Patrick tried the door. It was open. "I'll meet you back here in a minute."

He didn't wait for an answer, just stepped inside.

The post office was plain inside, with a well-swept hard plank floor and only a few government notices tacked to the walls, most of them yellow with age. Cubbyholes covered the back wall, where people from out of town would often get their post. The postmistress, a trim woman in her fifties who wore her hair up in a bun, ruled her kingdom from behind a tall walnut wood counter piled high with small brown parcels wrapped with string. Patrick wasn't sure of the woman's name yet, but she knew nearly everyone in town and their dog. Jack Duggan had even told him that she steamed personal letters open just to read them.

"No, she doesn't," Patrick had challenged his Australian friend when he had first heard the story.

"Yes, she does," argued Jack, but he hadn't been able to convince Patrick at the time.

Still, there was no doubt in Patrick's mind that Miss Hair-in-a-Bun knew all about him, about his paddle-steamer captain grandfather, about his mother, about his brother and sister, and possibly also about his father.

Maybe Pa tried to write another letter to Grandpa, he thought, stepping into the square lobby and clearing his throat. He was sure she would remember him from that letter, the one she had given him when he had first come to Echuca weeks ago, the one addressed to "Patrick McWaid." Of course, that letter had really been for his grandfather, who was also named Patrick, and it was the first real proof they'd had that their father was still alive.

"We're not open today," the postmistress declared without looking up from her mail.

"I'm sorry. The door was open."

The woman set a package down on the floor and looked sternly over her Benjamin Franklin spectacles, then smiled when she recognized Patrick.

"Oh, g'day." She winked at him. "Young Master McWaid, is it?"

"Yes, ma'am." He nodded politely. "I was just wondering if there might be any mail for me."

Or for Grandpa, he thought, but he didn't want to retell the story of how his grandfather had once used another man's name because he was ashamed of his prison past.

"Well, let's see. Abbott, Bromley, Cooper..."

Patrick watched her leaf through a stack of mail and tried to read the return addresses upside down. A couple of the letters were all the way from England, but most were from places like Sydney and Melbourne in Australia.

"I'm sorry." She finally adjusted her glasses. "But there's no mail today for Patrick McWaid."

"Oh." Patrick's face fell.

"Nice big package here for the Richardsons, though," she continued, as if that would make up for things. "They're originally from the Shepparton area. I believe Mr. Shepparton is married to a Johnson, but—oh, that reminds me, did I mention there was an odd fellow in the other day asking about you?"

Patrick froze at the news.

"Gave me a bit of a fright, I don't mind telling you," she went on, "just on account of his rough appearance. Looked like a government man, a prisoner, sure as you're alive."

"Oh?"

"Seemed to match the description, you know, a few weeks back, when we had that panic about the escaped convict lurking about. Well, wouldn't you know but that the constable's wife, Jane Fitzgerald, stepped in just then, and I told Janie that—"

"I'm sorry," Patrick interrupted her nonstop gossip when she paused for a breath, "but who was asking about a Patrick McWaid?"

She blinked. "Well, I can't exactly say, seeing as how we weren't formally introduced. But I can certainly tell you he looked a sight. I whispered to Janie to get her husband straight away, and that he should bring his revolver besides."

"Did he come?"

"Well, yes, but by then it was too late. The man left in quite a hurry."

"Red beard?"

"I believe so. Frightful character."

"And what did he want to know?"

The postmistress scratched her chin and searched the ceiling for answers.

"Well, now, I don't recall completely. I have to tell you I was quite a bit apprehensive, a little fearful of this character, and wasn't much listening to what he was saying. Not that he said much, mind you."

"So you don't remember anything he asked?"

She shook her head. "Could have been something about a letter he was expecting, or one he had sent, I'm not exactly sure. . . . Oh yes. Perhaps I shouldn't have, but I did mention to him there was a paddle-steamer captain by the name of McWaid, though he used to go by the name of Hughes, on account of—"

"Thank you!" Patrick had heard all he needed to know as he rushed out the door. *Pa! Right here in Echuca!*

CHAPTER 12

TO THE BARMAH FOREST

"I'm telling you, it's bound to come to no good," fumed the Old Man. "That weapon is going to hurt someone, sure as I'm standing here."

He stood in front of the prince's cannon with his arms crossed while Wilkinson emerged from behind the weapon with a satisfied look on his face.

"The cannon is perfectly safe, Captain," said the prince's assistant, writing down a few notes in his book. "And it lends a little something to the royal visit, don't you think?"

The Old Man shook his head, as if giving up, when he noticed Patrick returning. Becky disappeared inside to stow the supplies, followed by Michael.

"Patrick!" said his mother, who was sweeping the deck. "There you are. Disappearing again."

"He wasn't disappearing, Sarah," put in the Old Man. "I asked him to fetch a couple of things for us."

Patrick was breathless. "I stopped at the post office, Ma, and you'll never believe who was there—"

"I'm sorry," cut in his mother, opening up the door to the wheelhouse. "But could you possibly tell me later?"

"No, Ma, you don't understand. The postmistress said that she had seen Pa!"

Mrs. McWaid stopped her sweeping and looked at her son as if he had just dropped out of the sky.

"Your father?" she whispered. "How do you know? Are you sure?"

"Well, pretty sure. She didn't say 'John McWaid,' but she did say it was a man with a red beard."

Patrick explained everything the woman had said, but the Old Man didn't seem to believe what he was saying. Mrs. McWaid looked to the Old Man for advice.

"You don't think it could be John?" she asked.

He shrugged his shoulders and looked around cautiously.

"Doesn't seem likely," he answered, shaking his head. "And there's more than one man in the town with a red beard. I'm remembering the incident with the bushranger they dragged in, and then there'd be Scott Taylor at the hotel up the street, and . . ."

"But the woman at the post office said she didn't recognize him," insisted Patrick, not wanting to let go of the possibility.

The Old Man shook his head. "Aye, but what are we to do, lad? You think your father would be walking the streets of Echuca in broad daylight? Sure, that wouldn't be logical. Now, do we have all those flags up?"

Patrick sighed, and Wilkinson reappeared from the wheelhouse.

"Captain, I believe I'd like to test the cannon once more before we leave, just to ensure that it's completely—"

The Old Man held up his hands and shook his head. "Absolutely not. You've tested this infernal noisemaker quite enough already. I told you we'd be ready to take you up the river this morning, and ready we shall be. Is there anything else I can do for you, Mr. Wilkinson?"

Wilkinson shook his head and shrank back before he disappeared down the ladder to the main deck. As soon as he was out of sight, the Old Man turned back to them.

"When did the woman say she saw your pa?" he asked Patrick in a hushed voice.

Patrick finally understood. "Didn't want him to hear anything?"

The Old Man frowned and ignored the question. "When did she say?"

"She didn't say exactly *when* he came in. Just 'the other day,' I think."

"That could be two days or two weeks ago." The Old Man slapped his fist in the palm of his hand. "Still, what puzzles me is that if it really *was* your father, would he not have made his way here to the paddle steamer?"

The Old Man turned to Mrs. McWaid.

"All right, now, Sarah. I want you to keep your eyes and ears open to any rumors, and I want you to stay at the cabin up the river while I'm gone. We can drop you off."

"But wouldn't Pa be able to find us better if we were tied up here at the wharf?" asked Becky, who had come out to join them.

The Old Man shook his head. "You forget I have a schedule to meet, my dear lass. And now I've promised to take Prince Alfred and his party up the river."

"But, Captain," protested Patrick. He didn't want to leave on a trip up the river, either—not if there was a chance his father might show up at Erin's Landing, the captain's old riverfront cabin.

The Old Man lifted his eyebrow in warning. "Now, listen here, Sarah. I'll take the two older ones with me up the river to help out, and we'll drop you and Michael off at Erin's Landing. We'll only be a day or two, depending on how far this prince actually wants to travel. I'll be able to drop off my supplies at Yarrawonga, as well."

It was not a question; the Old Man obviously expected things to happen the way he said. Patrick nodded and turned away, his stomach clenched tight with worry.

CHAPTER 13

STORM ON THE MURRAY

Even though Patrick kept his fingers in his ears, he could feel the thump of the cannon blast against his chest. Birds scattered and shrieked as the *Lady Elisabeth* pulled slowly away from the Echuca wharf in the gathering gray.

"Aye, cleared up for now," the Old Man said as he poked his head out into the damp morning. "But I can tell you for a certainty that rain's going to be on us again before we get where we're going. Especially with the cannon."

"Oh, come now, Captain," Wilkinson shouted up from the lower deck. "You don't mean to tell me you believe those cloud-seeding cannons really work?"

"I'm not saying I believe it, and I'm not saying I don't believe it. All I'm saying is it's going to rain again. Cannon or no cannon. Pray cast your eye up at the sky, and you'll see the sense in what I'm sayin'."

Wilkinson looked up and nodded. "Well, then, sir, is this as fast as we go?"

The Old Man sucked in a breath through clenched teeth and said nothing. Echuca retreated slowly in the distance behind them.

"Patience, Wilkinson," Patrick heard the prince say as he stepped out on the deck to take advantage of the brief sunshine

89

between clouds. "You're always in a hurry to keep us on schedule. And we *are* on schedule."

"The *Lady E* may not be a'tall big, but she's one of the fastest boats on the Murray River," said the Old Man. "You won't get to where you want to go any quicker with someone else."

The prince smiled as they continued up the river. After they had dropped his mother and Michael off at the Old Man's cabin, Patrick noticed a lot more logs floating their direction. And he studied the dark clouds in the distance, waiting for the rain to hit them.

"The other thing that's going to slow us down is all the trees washing downriver," the Old Man told Patrick a few hours later. "I don't know why I agreed to this crazy excursion. We're going to be lucky if we're not holed."

"Did you say 'holed,' Captain?" Wilkinson asked as he stepped into the wheelhouse.

The Old Man closed his eyes for a moment before he answered. "No need to worry yourself in the least, Mr. Wilkinson. We left on time. And we've got things well under control."

Wilkinson returned to his notes, busily flipping pages. "I should hope so, Captain. Because at seven knots, and using this chart . . ."

The Old Man rolled his eyes and motioned for Patrick to take the wheel. Patrick looked quickly behind him to make sure his grandfather didn't mean a crewman.

"Me?"

The Old Man nodded. "You're seeing out of both eyes now, are you not? Keep to this side of the bends, see? The water is deeper over there. But there's plenty of water right now. Fact, if the water keeps rising like this, we'll be able to sail straight over the hills to Sydney."

"Oh, come now, Captain." Wilkinson checked his book. "I have written here that with the average rainfall for this time of year, we won't have to worry about flooding until the spring. That's months from now."

Patrick gripped the big wooden steering wheel and tried to keep to the side the Old Man had pointed out to him as they wound their way upriver.

"Nothing will be happening just the way you have it in your book." The Old Man marched Wilkinson to the window and pointed to the shore. "Is it supposed to be raining so much so early in the season? No. Is it supposed to be flooding? No again, young man. But this is the Murray River, not the River Thames back home in London, or wherever 'tis you come from. Here in Australia, you just take what comes."

What came next was a kettledrum downpour, so hard on the roof of the wheelhouse that they suddenly couldn't hear themselves speaking.

"See what I mean, sir?" shouted the Old Man. "Did your book say it was going to rain this hard today?"

"Well," stuttered Wilkinson. He closed his notebook carefully and stared out at the rain.

"Fact, I don't know that I've ever seen such a heavy downpour."

Patrick tried to see out ahead, but the rain had turned into a solid sheet of water, and it turned the river in front of them to foam.

"T'isn't all that bad, to be sure," the Old Man assured him. "Just remember to stay on the outside of the curves."

"But, Captain, I can't even see the curves."

"Well, then, you're doing fine, son. Probably have better eyes than I do, even with one of them as black as it is."

Patrick squinted, adjusted their course, and prayed he wouldn't lay them up into the muddy banks on either side—although he supposed it would be better to do something like that than to run into a log.

"Steer more to the left," commanded the Old Man, and Patrick obeyed, just as he felt a thump from below. The Old Man shook his head.

"Another log," he said, checking behind them. "I don't like this."

"Are you saying it's too dangerous to go on?" asked Wilkinson, pacing from side to side. "Are these logs going to delay our progress?"

It made Patrick dizzy just watching him. The Old Man grunted and finally took over the wheel.

"Can't see to steer because of the rain, the entire Barmah Forest is drifting down the river, and the water's rising even higher. Patrick, would you fetch my spectacles? They're on the shelf above my bunk, the one we've cleared off for the prince."

Patrick released the wheel with a sigh of relief. Like gusts of wind, the rain was still pouring and dumping, never letting up its powerful, wet attack. He had never seen such rain.

"Yes, sir." Patrick ran outside, down the ladder, and around the deck to the back door. By the time he made it inside, he was soaked to the skin.

"Spectacles, spectacles." He hadn't seen his grandfather wear glasses very much, but he guessed they would be needed on a day like today. From the main salon he heard the murmurs and occasional laughs of Prince Alfred and his friends; besides Wilkinson, he had brought along three other men. From down the hall Becky caught his eyes as she stepped out of the galley with a plate of food.

"You're all wet," she said, balancing the tray. He hurried after her, snatching a roast beef sandwich and cloth napkin. She tried to swing the tray away but wasn't quick enough.

"That's not for you," she scolded him, but he only smiled and wrapped up his prize in the napkin. It was a delicacy they had never eaten on the paddle steamer before, probably because they had nowhere to keep fresh meat.

"Might come in handy next time I get hungry," he told her as she disappeared around the corner. Patrick retreated back down the hall, stuffing the sandwich carefully in his loose back pocket. He tried the door to the Old Man's tiny room. Locked.

That's funny, he thought. *I can't remember him ever locking it before. Especially when he's upstairs.*

He tried again, wiggling the doorknob. "Hello?" he asked curiously, hoping no one would answer. "Is anyone in there?"

Maybe one of the prince's people is taking a nap, he decided. Then something clicked on the other side of the door, and it swung in a few inches.

"Come in here and shut the door," whispered a man's voice,

hoarse and hollow sounding. Patrick didn't recognize it and backed away.

"Excuse me," said Patrick, turning to go. "I'll come back later."

"No!" said the man, a little louder this time. "Patrick, that's you, isn't it?"

Patrick's knees nearly buckled at the sound of his name, and he stood shaking in the hallway. The voice was different, tired sounding and strained, but this time there was no mistake. It had to be him!

CHAPTER 14

STOWAWAY

"Pa?" Patrick croaked as he inched closer.

"Shh!" warned the man from behind the door. "Don't stand there talking in the hallway."

The cook, a stocky man named Albert, hurried by just then on his way to the salon with more food. He gave Patrick a suspicious look.

"You looking for something to do?" asked the cook. "Because if you are, your sister and I could use a little help serving these people the midafternoon meal. They're eating everything on board."

Patrick backed against the Old Man's door, his heart pounding through his chest. "No. I mean, yes. But I'm already helping the Old Man get his spectacles."

Albert frowned over his shoulder. "Yeh, well, you tell the Old Man I could use some more help once you finish with whatever it is you're doing."

Patrick nodded as he stepped backward into the Old Man's tiny sleeping room and latched the door behind him. The person he saw standing in the gray light from the single small window made him gasp.

"Pa . . ." He could only stare at the man in front of him, a shadow of the person his father had once been. A tangled red beard filled in sunken cheeks, and his usually short-trimmed curly red hair had grown wild, as well. And the laughing light brown eyes had been replaced by dull slivers, bloodshot and barely open. It had been almost half a year since Patrick had seen his father, back in the Kilmainham Jail in Dublin.

"I don't know why you're here, son," he croaked, his sunken eyes brimming with tears, "but I praise God you are."

"Pa!" Patrick wrapped his arms around his father and buried his face in the man's dirty, ripped shirt. It smelled of campfires and sweat.

"Careful there," said Mr. McWaid, resting his head on Patrick's and patting him on the back. "There's not much left of me to squeeze."

With that, Patrick's father backed away and launched into a hacking, dry cough. He held his sides and grimaced in pain.

"Pa, you're sick."

Mr. McWaid shook his head and cleared his throat. "Just a wee cough. I've had worse. Now, you tell me what is going on and how I find you here in Australia, all the way from Dublin?"

A knock at the door interrupted him, and he shrank back into the corner at the sound, behind the Old Man's bunk.

"Patrick, are you in there?" asked his sister. "Who are you talking to?"

Patrick unlatched the door without answering, cracked it open, and grabbed Becky's wrist.

"What are you—" she began, stumbling inside, but her reaction was the same as Patrick's when she saw her father standing in front of her.

"Oh, Pa," she gasped and gave her father a long hug. He stroked her hair, and the tears came fast for all three.

"Don't squeeze him too much," warned Patrick. "I think his ribs hurt from coughing. He's sick."

"Let's not talk about that now." Their father coughed as if to demonstrate to his daughter how sick he was. "You're here, and it's beyond me to understand how this has all happened. But where is your mother?"

Patrick looked over at Becky, who was still holding on to their father. "She went to the cabin with Michael this morning, Pa."

"Oh." Their father's face fell. "The cabin?"

"We'll explain everything when you see Grandpa." Becky took his hand, but he pulled back.

"I can't go out there, kids." He shook his head and lowered his voice. "You don't know how dangerous it is for me to be seen."

"Pa, we know all about Burke." Patrick wiped his eyes dry. "We've seen him, and we know how he tried to have you killed."

"You know that?" Their father looked from face to face, as if he was trying to drink in every detail.

"We even know about the letter you sent your father, and we know you've been looking for him for months. We just don't know how you finally found him—I mean, us."

Patrick still wasn't quite sure if he was imagining things or if his father was real. *If this is a dream*, he finally decided, *then I want to stay asleep as long as I can*.

Their father opened and closed his mouth a couple of times, then sank down into the Old Man's bed before he went on. "I've prayed every night since I escaped that I would at least find my father before they captured me again."

"But how did you end up here?" wondered Becky.

"I finally decided I had to take a chance in town, had to ask someone if they knew of Patrick McWaid. I'd sent a letter weeks ago, you see, and . . ." His voice trailed off.

Patrick grinned. "You gave the lady at the post office a good scare."

"You heard about that, eh? Well, it was worth it to find you. I never imagined . . ."

"We came after you, Pa," explained Becky, and she launched into a quick story about how they had made it to Australia.

Patrick couldn't wait for her to finish. "I'm going upstairs to tell him you're here." Patrick jumped up and down in excitement.

"Well, then, I'm going to get Pa something to eat," added Becky.

Patrick carefully checked the hallway before slipping out. In the salon the prince and his guests were carrying on as they had been before, laughing and generally ignoring the steady rain outside. It wasn't quite as heavy as earlier, but now the water was finding its way in through cracks in the ceiling, leaving dozens of puddles on the floor. A tree scraped past outside, and Patrick had to step back from the edge of the deck to avoid being snagged by the branches. Upstairs in the wheelhouse, someone was arguing.

". . . and I'm telling you it doesn't matter," said Wilkinson, leaning against the side door. He ignored Patrick when he walked in. "We're paying you well for this excursion, remember. And I've already told you that we'll pay for any damage to your little boat."

"Little boat?" The Old Man's cheek's puffed out red, like a man playing the tuba, while he kept his eyes on the river ahead. "It's not the little boat I'm so worried about. It's the lives aboard her. How much sterling is it you want to pay for *them*?"

"Oh, come now, Captain. It can't be as dangerous as all that. Everyone told us you're an expert on this river."

A drop of rain found its way through the ceiling, catching Wilkinson on the forehead. He winced and dried himself with a handkerchief.

"All I'm saying," huffed the Old Man, "is that we're running into snags all the time now. Logs, as well, cut by the lumber operation upriver. They're like battering rams, I'm telling you. One of these times it's not going to bounce off the hull but—"

Another branch scraped by, making his point.

"You see what I mean?" The Old Man leaned on his wheel slowly, bringing them around the next bend. "It's time to turn around."

"Well, now, I'm sure I can't explain why, but His Majesty has his heart set on seeing this Barmah Forest of yours, and see it he shall. Can't we lay up for the evening a little farther upstream? I see on the chart here . . ."

The Old Man frowned, and it looked as if he had lost the argument.

"Captain?" Patrick saw his chance to interrupt. "There's someone—"

"Did you bring up my spectacles the way I asked you?" snapped the Old Man. "I thought you'd disappeared."

"Oh, the spectacles." Patrick swallowed. "I forgot."

"You're gone fifteen minutes and you forgot? Whatever were you doing, lad?"

"Oh, now, Captain," said Wilkinson. "Don't be too gruff with the boy."

"You stay out of this." The Old Man wiped at the glass in front of him with the sleeve of his jacket. "Patrick, I asked you to fetch my spectacles, and for a fact that's what I meant."

"I'm sorry, Grandfather, but there's really something you need to see down in your room. It's urgent."

The Old Man jerked his head around to glare at Patrick, and Wilkinson took the chance to disappear downstairs. "You're going to need a very good explanation for this, because we're in the middle of a storm. . . ."

His voice trailed off to nothing as the rain continued to pelt down. Patrick turned to see his father standing on the side wing of the deck, just outside the wheelhouse, staring at the Old Man.

"Hello, Father." John McWaid managed to whisper above the sound of the rain and the water.

Looking almost embarrassed, the Old Man turned for a second back to the river, but Patrick stepped up next to him at the wheel.

"Johnny?" croaked the Old Man. He squared his shoulders and cleared his throat. "Excuse me. For a moment there, you reminded me of someone I once knew. Who are you?"

"It *is* him, Grandpa," said Becky, stepping into the wheelhouse.

The Old Man, stunned, looked up and down at his son, but he shook his head. "You're not him," he argued. "You can't be him. I don't know you."

Patrick took the wheel as his grandfather stepped aside. Mr. McWaid, looking even more like a skeleton in the full gray light of the afternoon, stepped up to the Old Man and put his hands on his father's shoulders.

"My name is John Martin McWaid," he said steadily. "I was born in Dublin the seventeenth of January, 1830. My mother's name was Elisabeth McWaid. My father's name was—is—Patrick McWaid. He was taken to Australia as a prisoner when I was a boy, and I never saw him again. Or I hadn't, until just now."

The Old Man's hand started to shake, and he tried to steady himself by holding his chin, but it did no good. His hand moved to his forehead, and his shoulders picked up the shaking. In a moment he was sobbing, holding his forehead, looking up at the ghost from his past. His own son.

"Johnny," he sobbed, and Patrick was almost embarrassed to look at his grandfather. "The only thing I recognize is that curly red hair. You were just a lad when I left. No older than . . . than Patrick here."

"I always knew my red hair would be good for something." Mr. McWaid stepped up to the Old Man and put out his hand. "Thirty years is a long time."

" 'Tis that." The captain nodded his head and took a deep breath before he took his son's outstretched hand. "But welcome to Australia, Johnny."

For a moment the two men embraced, but the Old Man pulled back.

"But what's happened to you? Fit an' well you're not."

Mr. McWaid bowed his head and coughed. "Been on the run for a few months, now. Was almost killed on the prison ship. I found out that Burke had bribed the guards, all except for two who helped me escape."

"That was when you escaped on another ship?" asked Becky.

Her father nodded. "The people on the ship who helped me escape from Fremantle were kind, to be sure, but it was too dangerous for them to hide me very long. So I slipped off the vessel before they made Adelaide, thinking that I had to find you somehow."

"That you did." The Old Man shook his head, listening to the story.

"I've been hiding in the bush ever since, getting food when I can, trying to stay out of sight. Some of the aborigines helped."

"All this way, Johnny. But you're safe with us now."

Mr. McWaid smiled weakly and looked around. "I never meant to put you in danger, Father. But I think I was seen coming aboard, during all the shouting as you were getting ready to leave. I'm not sure."

"Who would have seen you?" asked Patrick. "The constable?"

Mr. McWaid shook his head. "No, I can't be certain, but I thought I saw Conrad Burke back in Echuca. He's been—"

"Him again?" The Old Man's cheeks started to redden, as they had with Wilkinson. His hands knotted into fists.

"You know Burke?" asked Patrick's father, giving the Old Man a questioning look.

"Aye, we've met, once. He's quite the persistent one."

"He's the bad dream that won't go away," added Becky.

Their father put up his hands. "Well, now, I said I'm not absolutely certain it was him who saw me. But I *am* certain I can't go on running like this. Perhaps I was wrong to escape in the first place."

"But you weren't wrong!" insisted Patrick as he followed a bend in the river. It seemed to be widening out for a stretch.

Becky nodded her agreement. "We know what they were trying to do to you!"

"Ah!" cried the Old Man. He waved his hand and stepped back from a steady stream of rainwater that suddenly found a way through the roof and poured onto his head. "I don't understand exactly what they were trying to do to you, Johnny, but I *can* tell you what the rain is going to do to this boat if we don't plug the leaks."

Everyone laughed except Mr. McWaid, who smiled and searched his father's eyes.

"I must know one thing, though, Father," said Mr. McWaid.

The Old Man nodded and crossed his arms.

"Why did you never write me back? You know I wrote to you for years and years while you were still a prisoner."

The Old Man's expression turned as dark as the clouds outside.

"Did you never get any of the letters?" asked Mr. McWaid.

Tears returned to the Old Man's eyes, and he nodded sadly.

"I remember when I was growing up." Patrick's father blinked and looked up, as if trying to pull back a memory. "People would always ask me about my father. 'What happened to your pa, lad?' And I would just tell them he disappeared at sea. . . ."

The Old Man crossed his arms as tears began to run down his cheeks. Finally he pointed Becky to a cabinet behind the steering wheel.

"Open it, Becky," he commanded her. "Bottom shelf."

Becky stooped and pulled out what appeared to be a small box stuffed full of old letters. She pulled one out, and as Patrick had guessed, it was addressed in his father's steady handwriting to "Mr. Patrick McWaid."

"Every one I saved while I was serving out my time," the Old Man finally admitted. "Until you finally stopped writing, years ago."

"Oh, Pa," said Mr. McWaid. "I wish you would have answered instead of just saving the letters."

"I do, too." The Old Man brushed aside another tear with the sleeve of his shirt. "I do, too, son. But I was too . . . ashamed, or pig-headed, or both. I'm sorry."

Patrick's father shook his head. "I've heard enough. You don't have to explain any more just yet."

"Oh, aye, indeed I do." The Old Man held up his hand, once again in command. "I've apologized to Patrick and Rebecca. Now I owe you an apology, Johnny, for letting you down all these years. If I could do it over again . . ."

"No use in that." Patrick's father put his hand on the Old Man's shoulder. "It's past."

" 'Tis that." The Old Man cleared his throat. "But now . . ."

Patrick couldn't help himself. "But now what are we to do?"

Everyone looked at him as if he had interrupted a pastor's sermon or a symphony orchestra.

"Now that we've found him," Patrick continued, "what will we do? Pa's still an outlaw!"

The Old Man chewed on his lip for a moment before turning to Mr. McWaid.

"The youngsters are right," he agreed, pointing a crooked finger at his son. "We're going to do something about this situation. Perhaps get you out of Australia. But now ye must tell me straight, as I've told you. Did you do anything to have the law after you?"

Patrick's father shook his head slowly but surely. "Never. I would never do anything that would dishonor my family."

Someone cleared his throat out on the deck, and they all turned to see the duke of Edinburgh standing on the upper deck. Wilkinson stood right beside him, holding an umbrella.

"Excuse me?" asked the prince, eyeing Mr. McWaid. "I was simply curious about the operation of the vessel."

Wilkinson looked sourly to the side as he pulled down the umbrella and shook off the water before he stepped inside. The rain, it seemed, was a personal insult.

"Ah yes . . ." The Old Man hesitated a moment.

"If it's not inconvenient," said the prince. He glanced again at Patrick and Becky's father, then stepped around him to look at the compass and the wheel, where Patrick was still steering.

"Unusual chart," said the prince, looking down at the map of the river, stretched between two rollers like a scroll. The Old Man showed him where they were on the river.

"Boomerang Bend coming up," he told them, his finger on the chart. As far as Patrick could tell, Boomerang Bend was a wide spot in the river with an island in the middle. "At least, I think that's it up there in the rain. Nearly underwater in this flood. Hard to tell— some of the banks are washed out. We'll pass on the right."

"Does it always rain this hard?" asked the prince. "Wilkinson promised me the rains would be quite light this time of the year if it rained at all. And all those logs. You didn't tell me about those, Wilkinson."

The Old Man leaned over Patrick's shoulder and indicated where he should steer. Suddenly he stiffened, and Patrick strained to see through the rain. In less time than it took to realize what it was, a wicked-looking giant log jumped out of the water to face them head on.

CHAPTER 15

AGROUND

"Hard right, Patrick!" shouted the Old Man, and in the split second of confusion, Patrick obeyed by turning to the left. But there was no time to kick himself for the mistake; the impact shook the paddle steamer as nothing else ever had. They all heard the sickening crunch, the sound of splintering wood forward and below. If he didn't know better, Patrick would have guessed that the log torpedo had crushed the entire front end of the *Lady Elisabeth*.

The battering-ram impact threw the prince and Wilkinson to their knees with a surprised shout, while Becky grabbed her father for balance and the Old Man fell to the floor next to Patrick, who was still gripping the wheel. Whatever had happened, Patrick knew instantly it was not a small hole in the hull. Within seconds he could feel the weight of the river pouring in, as if the *Lady Elisabeth* were a whale that had opened its mighty jaws wide for a drink.

"For the shore, Patrick!" commanded the Old Man from the floor. "Beach it on the shore to the right!"

Patrick struggled with the wheel, but it seemed locked in place.

"It . . . it won't turn," Patrick replied as he leaned on the wheel with all his weight. He tried desperately to get the boat turned back in the direction the Old Man had commanded. "Something's jammed!"

"Here, watch out, now." The Old Man pulled on the wheel from the floor and rose to his feet. But even with his extra weight, he couldn't budge the wheel.

"Branches must have jammed the rudder." The Old Man looked out through the rain as the nose of the *Lady E* started to dip under the current. It wasn't far to either bank of the Murray River, not far at all, but they were locked in a deadly straight course—straight down to the bottom of the river.

"I say, what is happening?" asked the prince, struggling to his feet. Even over the sound of the grinding and crashing of the dying paddle steamer, they could hear shouts from below, and the sound of shattering dishes as nearly everything breakable on board dumped off its shelves. The two paddles, one on each side, still churned up the river.

"We're sinking like a rock is what's happening!" Wilkinson leaped out onto the tilting deck, his voice up to a panicked pitch. "We're all going to drown in this wretched river!"

"Captain!" The crewman named Prentice stumbled out on deck, just below them. "The water is—"

"Aye," the Old Man growled a reply as he wrestled the wheel, still jammed securely in place. "I can see plainly what's happening."

The prince gripped the door, his face white with fright, as Patrick's father jumped to help turn the wheel.

"The island's up ahead!" said Patrick, looking up. A wave of river water washed over the forward deck, and they rocked dangerously forward once more. The island seemed like their only chance before the *Lady Elisabeth* dove with frightening speed under the water. Patrick jumped on the wheel with his father and grandfather. A sickening *crack* came from below the deck, and the wheel spun free, sending the two adults to the floor again. Patrick saw the island—not much more than a bald sandbar with a couple of low bushes barely poking above the unforgiving river—up ahead and slightly to the left. It was squarely in the middle of the rising river.

"Left," grunted Patrick, pointing the paddle steamer at the washed-out point of the island. "Lord, please get us there. Just a little bit more."

Like an out-of-control rocking horse, the front of the ship

lurched up again, then dipped below the water one last time. With a bone-wrenching shudder, the *Lady Elisabeth* came to a sudden stop and dug into the sand. The steam engine wheezed and died, leaving them with only the sound of the pounding rain and the gurgling river filling the *Lady Elisabeth*'s hull.

"Out, out, out!" ordered the Old Man, his voice booming with authority. He didn't have to look outside to know what had happened, just grabbed Patrick and Becky like a mother cat with a couple of kittens. "You with us, Johnny?"

Mr. McWaid rolled over on the floor, coughing and wide-eyed, but he nodded. Prince Alfred was already out the door, but he returned to help Patrick's father to his feet. Without a look back to help anyone, Wilkinson was down the ladder and racing down the deck. The paddle steamer rolled to the left, tilting the ladder at a crazy angle—making it even harder to get down.

"Pa, can you make it?" asked Becky.

Their father nodded but slipped and hung for a long moment before pulling himself back up.

"Here," said the prince, pulling Mr. McWaid along by the arm. "Just a little farther."

By this time the forward deck was underwater, even though they had jammed themselves up against the sandbar island. The men who had come with the prince held on to the upper railing of the tilting ship while one of the Old Man's crew members tried to calm them.

"What's going to happen to us?" An older gentleman grabbed the Old Man's jacket as he slid down the last rung of the ladder. "I say, what's—"

"It's all right, Mr. Franklin," said the prince, stepping over to help. "I'm sure the captain has faced much worse calamities, haven't you, Captain?"

The Old Man nodded as he pried the man's hands loose. "Just a bit of bad luck. Water's not deep. We'll get to shore in a few minutes and look things over from there."

"But what about the *Lady Elisabeth*?" asked Patrick.

As if to answer his question, a wave of cold water surged in through the door and swept over the floor, ankle deep.

"That's it," cried the Old Man. "Everyone out to the rear deck, away from the water."

Can we swim to shore? wondered Patrick. He knew it wasn't really so far, but with the water rising, and with his sick father . . .

Patrick and Becky each took one of their father's arms as he stumbled back with them to the safety of the rear deck, away from the rising water that now covered the salon floor.

"We need to tie her off," shouted Prentice. The Old Man paused before shaking his head.

"We do, but there's nothing on the island strong enough to tie to. No trees, nothing."

As he spoke, the *Lady Elisabeth* lurched in the current, turning and bumping, but again they held fast to something.

"I'm going to swim for it," announced Wilkinson, looking out the window. "This thing will be our coffin."

"We're still safe for now," the Old Man barked in his face. "And you're not going anywhere until I give the word. Y'understand me?"

Wilkinson looked out at the water, swallowed, and nodded.

"And we'll all get to shore," added the Old Man in a softer voice, "if we just keep our wits about us. Now, Prentice, we need a line to the shore. Then we'll pull ourselves over in the boat."

"The boat?" asked Wilkinson.

"That's what I said," replied the Old Man, looking around the deck.

Wilkinson backed away slowly.

"Where *is* the boat, Grandpa?" asked Patrick.

The Old Man clenched his fists and stared at the prince's aide. "You know something about this, Mr. Wilkinson?"

"I . . . I had it moved to make room for some of our supplies," Wilkinson managed to whisper. "I'm thinking perhaps it wasn't replaced before we left. There were just too many things to think about. It isn't my fault!"

No one said anything else. But as the *Lady Elisabeth* creaked and groaned, Prentice scurried to find a long coil of thin line with a weight on the end, the kind that sailors used to throw between ships.

"Problem is," he grunted as he swung it back and forth before letting the weighted end go, "who's going to catch it, even if I *can* get it to shore?"

Patrick looked from one shore to the other, at the tall eucalyptus trees that lined both sides, and at the sandbar that held them in place right in the middle of the river.

"Why does it have to widen out here, of all places?" wondered Prentice.

"It's all my fault," mumbled Patrick.

"Excuse me," replied the deckhand, recoiling the rope for another throw, "but I don't think you had anything to do with this, Master Patrick."

"You don't understand. I was steering. Grandpa said to go right, and I went left. Then the rudder jammed, and we rammed right into the island instead of the shore like we should have."

"Can't be helped." Prentice dismissed him with a wave of his hand. "Right now our only worry is getting a line to safety."

The little crowd cheered when Prentice made one more try, but again his line only splashed in the water just short of the shore, and he pulled it back in.

"It's no use, Captain," he finally said. "The only way it will work is if we can wrap it around a tree. I just can't throw it that far. Maybe I should swim for it."

"No!" boomed the Old Man.

The paddle steamer shifted again, and they all scrambled to keep their balance on the deck. No one seemed to care anymore that it was still raining and they were soaking wet. Becky held her father up. He coughed and wobbled uncertainly.

"You must see a doctor when we get back to town," the prince told him, and Patrick's father nodded politely. "I'll have Wilkinson make the arrangements. Wilkinson?"

The prince's aide was nowhere on the deck.

"I saw him go forward," Becky told her brother, and Patrick ran back up to find the man.

"Mr. Wilkinson!" shouted Patrick, and he stopped when he came to the opposite side, out of view of everyone. "What are you doing?"

The water washed over the deck almost up to their knees, so cold that it first made his feet tingly, then numb. He wiggled his toes to keep the blood circulating. Wilkinson hung halfway over the railing. He had slipped off his black leather shoes and carried a coil of thick rope over his shoulder.

"I am not going to die here on this river!" the man insisted, and the look on his face reminded Patrick of a scared animal.

"But the captain said not to do anything alone," said Patrick, sliding over to Wilkinson and grabbing his arm. "That rope is just going to weigh you down. It's too thick."

Wilkinson jerked back his arm and backhanded Patrick across the face, catching his knuckles on Patrick's mouth and sending Patrick tumbling backward.

"No!" Patrick yelled as he fell, but Wilkinson paid no attention. Before Patrick could get to his feet, the man had disappeared into the river opposite of where Prentice had been trying to throw his rope.

"Captain!" yelled Patrick, rushing as fast as he could back to the rear deck. "Your Highness! Wilkinson just jumped overboard!"

Still clutching his coil of rope, Wilkinson drifted quickly by the *Lady Elisabeth*. When they saw him, they all waved and shouted, but he appeared to ignore their shouts as he paddled desperately with his one free hand. Instead of crossing the river, though, he was only swept farther downstream, nearly straight behind them.

"Pull the rope back!" someone suggested, and two of the men from the prince's group rushed back to the rope, which had been tied loosely to the railing. But by the time they were able to pull any of it back, Wilkinson had long since let go of his end and disappeared down the river, paddling weakly.

"There's the end of it," said one of the men, holding up the dripping rope.

Patrick reached for his mouth. His hand came back bloody from where Wilkinson had hit him. No one else had noticed in the stunned silence.

"I don't believe I've ever known him to be a strong swimmer," the prince finally declared. He stared out at the river and shook his head. "Why did he do such a thing?"

"Perhaps he thought he could tie it to a tree on the shore," the Old Man told the prince, then turned to the others. "But now listen to me, all of you. We're all going to get off this paddle steamer, but we have to work together and not do anything else foolish."

"But Wilkinson!" protested one of the men, still staring down the river.

"He'll be all right," the Old Man tried to reassure them once again. "And so will we."

"But your man can't even throw the rope to the shore, it's so flooded," piped up one of the prince's friends. "And while we sit here together, we're going to be washed down the river!"

The Old Man frowned.

"Captain, I hesitate to mention this," added Prince Alfred, "but it looks as if our island is almost underwater."

CHAPTER 16

RESCUE AT BOOMERANG BEND

Patrick and the others looked forward—sure enough, the rain-swollen river was starting to wash over their sandbar island. Only the low covering of bushes still remained above the rising river.

"Some island," said Patrick. He leaned against the three-foot cannon, trying to think. "Where is The Great Philippe when you really need him?"

Becky pushed the wet hair out of her face and squinted at her brother.

"What did you say?"

Patrick only shook his head. "Nothing, Becky. I was just thinking about the tightrope act."

"Exactly." She smiled and ran her hand across the cannon. "Grandpa, I think I know how we can get a rope to the trees."

"Not now, Rebecca," the Old Man grunted as he tried to heave their line toward shore. But like Prentice, he was always just short of the goal.

"But, Grandfather, I think this might work."

The Old Man sighed and threw his rope down. The *Lady Elisabeth* teetered still farther.

"I think we ought to swim for it," suggested another man.

The Old Man scowled at the suggestion. "What, and end up like like your friend Wilkinson? No one is going into that water."

"Look," said Becky, holding on to the cannon. "This cannon works, doesn't it?"

"I'm afraid Wilkinson was the only one who knew how to set it off," said the prince. "It was rather his hobby."

"Well, we can figure it out." Becky was determined. "All we have to do is stuff the rope in there and shoot it at the trees."

Even Patrick frowned. "But, Becky, this is just a toy. For making noise, not for shooting things."

"But it *could* work, couldn't it?"

"I . . . I don't know." Prince Alfred shook his head uncertainly. "I don't think so."

"But isn't that the way they shoot harpoons now?" she persisted. "With a little cannon just like this?"

The Old Man scratched his head. "She's right about that. Maybe it's worth a try."

Becky grabbed her brother's hand, and they rushed into the salon.

"Where did he put the gunpowder?" she asked.

"Probably on the deck where it's underwater by now."

"Oh, come on. Help me look."

Patrick finally found a small bag of something floating near the back door.

"I think this is it," he called to Becky. "It smells. But it's all wet, like everything else."

Becky took the dripping sack from his hands and opened it.

"Maybe not *all* wet." She dug carefully through the bag. "The powder in the middle is still dry, I think."

Back on the rear deck, the Old Man had carefully coiled up the thin line once again, and he took the powder from her.

"This is either going to work," he told them, "or we're going to blow ourselves up in the process."

"I don't think it's ever been fired like this," warned the prince.

The Old Man looked grim as Becky helped him pour in dry power, followed by a handful of nails, and finally the rolled-up end of the heaving line, which was attached to a small anchor the Old Man dug out of a dirty storage locker in the back of the boat. He packed it all in, then pointed the cannon at the nearest line of branches.

"Now matches," said the Old Man.

"I have some." The same man who had nearly jumped into the water after Wilkinson stepped forward and held out a small metal matchbox. Everyone stopped their nervous chatter as the Old Man took the matches and struck once, then twice.

"Too wet," he mumbled, taking another match. It broke in his hand. A third and a fourth match fizzled, too, until finally the fifth one took hold and blazed. Everyone who could see cheered while Patrick and Becky did their best to keep the rain from getting the match wet.

"All right, stand back," commanded the Old Man, and they held their ears.

The fuse on the bottom of the cannon sputtered and sparked as it caught fire, then burned low in a weak puff of smoke. Patrick held his breath, waiting. He bit the end of his thumb to keep from saying anything. Nothing happened.

"Aww . . ." began Patrick, taking a step toward the cannon, but his grandfather held him back.

"Not yet!" warned the Old Man, but the fuse was now burned out. He blew out his cheeks and looked at Becky.

"Well, it was a good i—"

The cannon's explosion sent Patrick to the deck, falling back on his father. Everyone else reeled in shock, unprepared for the boom, and the rope whistled from its coil on the deck and through the air.

"We did it!" The Old Man smiled for the first time. Patrick helped his father to his feet. Mr. McWaid's face looked as ashen as the dark clouds overhead, and his red hair was plastered to his head.

"Pa, we have to get you to a doctor." Patrick reached up to feel his father's forehead in the way he remembered his mother doing for him many times when he was little. It was burning.

"All right, let's see what we can do with this lifeline." The Old Man pulled back on the heaving line to make sure it wasn't coming loose from its roost in the trees, where the anchor had tangled. "I don't think it's strong enough to hold much weight."

"Then I'm going across." Becky picked up the end of a stronger rope and tied it around her waist.

"Oh no, you don't," objected Patrick.

"Becky, wait," said Mr. McWaid, but the effort to talk seemed to be almost too much for him.

"I'm only half the weight of any of you," she insisted.

"Except me," Patrick corrected her.

Becky ignored the comment and hiked up the men's pants she wore under her dress. When Patrick stared at her, she set her jaw defensively.

"I just thought perhaps they'd come in handy, is all, if I had to do a little work. And, look, I'll even wear a safety loop." She tied another short length of rope around her waist, then up and around the heaving line. Patrick didn't want to imagine what would happen if the line snapped.

"But, Becky, it's not much more than a clothesline," he tried once more, just as the *Lady E* squirmed in the current.

"We don't have time to argue about this," she said, tightening the knot around her waist and stepping up to the railing.

"I can't let you do this, Rebecca," said the Old Man, looking nervously from Becky to Mr. McWaid. His son was shivering, his eyes closed.

"But, Grandpa, you know it's our best chance."

The Old Man sighed and lifted her higher, then checked the knot on her safety loop himself. Without another word, she looped her legs around the thin line and launched out over the water, an upside-down inchworm only a few feet above the churning, angry waters of the Murray.

Slowly, steadily, Becky made her way across the river, pausing a couple of times to rest. At one point the line looked as if it might snap, it was stretched so thin, and she nearly brushed the water.

"Almost there, Becky!" Patrick shouted. "Keep moving."

She paused for a better grip, but her right hand slipped, then the other. A second later she was hanging with her head and shoulders nearly bobbing in the water.

"Becky!" croaked their father. "Hold on!"

Patrick stood helplessly on the deck, wanting to fly or pull the rope back in, *anything*, but he couldn't. Becky's safety loop held tight, but still she was upside down, needing to pull herself back up.

"Pull!" Patrick told her, not sure if he could have done it himself if he were out there. "Pull back up, Becky!"

Becky bobbed up, grasping at but missing the rope above her. After a second try, and a third, she was still hanging helplessly.

One more time, Becky. . . . Patrick prayed for his sister as she struggled, until finally her fingers clamped around the rope and she brought herself back up. Only a few more feet, and she inched her way to shore. Minutes later, she stood on the other side and waved at them, rope in hand.

"She made it!" cried the Old Man. "Good girl!"

Without delay, Patrick and the Old Man threaded the end of their new rope through a large wooden pulley, the kind the river men used for pulling cargo in and out of their boats or pulling big loads across the deck. As big as a loaf of bread, the well-oiled metal wheel spun easily.

"Here, let's hook this block up to a harness of some sort," said the Old Man.

"Block?" The prince, watching them closely, didn't understand.

"Block. Pulley. Same thing. We'll need a French bowline, Patrick."

Patrick nodded, trying to remember all the knots he had learned at sea on their long voyage to Australia. The French bowline made a double loop, one beneath his legs, then behind his back. . . .

"Good." The Old Man grabbed the two loops from Patrick and strung them up to their pulley. He motioned for a man from the group to step up.

"You expect me to . . ." The man's voice trailed off, and he held his tall stovepipe hat closely to his chest. Quickly, the Old Man took the hat and flung it into the river. The man stuttered a protest, but the Old Man calmly looped the harness over him.

"I'm sorry," he told him, "but we have no time for hats this trip, sir. I want you to get to safety. Now, kindly step down into this second loop, and we'll make it tight. Jump when I say."

Patrick waved at his sister across the water, holding the end of the thin line that had carried her across as if she was ready for a tug-of-war. She waved back, ready.

"Hold on!" cried the Old Man, half pushing the man out across the water.

Becky pulled him across in a matter of seconds, and they repeated the process for the other passengers, then for Prince Alfred and their grandfather's two crewmen, Prentice and Albert. At last it was just Patrick and his father and the Old Man. The captain of the *Lady Elisabeth* looked around one last time. The ship looked sadder than ever, still decked out in soggy flags and bunting.

"It was my fault," said Patrick under his breath.

The Old Man turned on him. "I don't want to hear that ever again. Wasn't your fault the rudder jammed or the log poked a hole in the hull. Now, get in that harness."

Patrick obeyed, but when he looked at his father, he stepped back out.

"How are we going to get Pa across? He can't hold on for himself."

His father opened his eyes and struggled to his feet, coughing. "I can . . . make it."

He convinced no one, but Patrick looped the rope over his father's back and up around his legs, tightening the rope as much as he dared.

"Pull hard, Becky!" he shouted, knowing his father couldn't balance for long and that he might flip over on his head like a rag doll at any moment.

Halfway across, something jerked, and Mr. McWaid suddenly dunked in the water before the line stretched tight again, almost too tight.

"The *Lady Elisabeth* is pulling loose!" Patrick yelled at his father as he jerked on toward shore, somehow managing to hang on. At the end of the rope, strong hands pulled Patrick's father to safety just a few paces from where the water lapped ever higher.

Patrick looked around at the *Lady Elisabeth*, which now seemed like an anchor in the middle of the river. The little island was gone, completely covered by water.

"You're next, lad," his grandfather said as Patrick tightened the ropes around himself. There was no arguing, of course, only a panicked feeling as his feet dragged in the water and the *Lady E* started to slip even more.

Becky grabbed him around the waist, and they both tumbled into the mud when he made it safely across.

"Thanks, sis."

"No time for that." Becky ripped the ropes off Patrick, and they sent the pulley back across one last time. The rope tightened and slacked as the paddle steamer slid slowly backward.

"He's not going to make it," whispered Prentice, but Patrick wouldn't listen. He and Becky stood ready at the end of the line, digging their heels in, waiting for the Old Man to climb into the loops and signal he was ready.

"Pull!" shouted Patrick, just as his grandfather's arm went up. Patrick felt someone else behind him, and he glanced back for a moment to see his father, his face drawn in pain.

"Pa, you—"

"Pull, Patrick!"

The Old Man nearly flew from his stricken ship just as the current caught it and twirled it like a top. The rope on their end held fast, while the end tied to the *Lady Elisabeth* ripped away a section of railing. The Old Man was dumped into the river and disappeared like a stone.

CHAPTER 17

APPROACHING THUNDER

"Help us!" shouted Patrick. "Everyone pull!"

The prince was the first to grab the rope behind him, then the others. Together they dug their heels into the muddy bank and battled the river for the life of the Old Man.

"Oh!" Becky slipped to her back but quickly scrambled to her feet. They pulled, hand over hand, even as they climbed backward up the bank.

Pull, pull, Patrick told himself as they yanked the last few feet of rope. It had seemed an eternity, but the tug-of-war probably lasted less than a minute before they finally saw the form of the Old Man roll up out of the muddy water.

At the head of the line, Patrick and Becky were the first to drop their hold and jump to his side. He was sputtering and panting, too weak to get to his knees.

"Grandpa!" cried Becky. "Are you all right?"

With Patrick's help, she rolled him over and helped him sit up, but he only looked out at the river to check on the *Lady Elisabeth*.

"Never felt better." He leaned on his granddaughter to get to his feet. "But I wanted to get a couple more lines on the *Lady E* before she washed down the river."

The paddle steamer was half underwater, a few hundred yards downstream from where she had broken loose from the island, and tilted even more to the side. A pileup of logs and tree branches held the ship in place, its bright red, white, and blue bunting still bobbing around in the water.

"We can't go out there again," said Patrick's father, breathing hard. He tried to say something else, then crumpled to his knees and fell to the ground.

"Get him up here!" ordered the Old Man, again in charge. Patrick and Becky turned their attention from their grandfather to their father, dragging him up to shelter and a soft bed of eucalyptus leaves under a protective canopy of trees. Patrick stumbled but never let go of his father's shoulders.

"Well, it's not completely dry," pronounced the Old Man after everyone had settled down in the sweet-smelling eucalyptus leaves a couple of hours later. The rain had settled to a steady drizzle, and Patrick guessed it was about dinnertime. "But it's soft, and we could be in a much worse predicament."

"Hear, hear," agreed the prince. "I must say we're grateful to you, Captain, for your quick action out there."

"Indeed, you should be thanking the girl," replied the Old Man. "If it wasn't for her . . ."

"Quite," agreed the prince. "I shall. I'll see to it that we get some assistance with recovering your ship, as well. But right now we must send someone out to find Wilkinson."

"Or his body," added one of the men. "The crazy fool deserves it."

"We'll have none of that," snapped the prince. "Wilkinson has been a loyal aide ever since I was a boy. He merely panicked, that's all, which is something you should all keep in mind not to do. Montgomery and Chambers, kindly make your way along the river and see what you can find. Surely he's still alive."

"As you say, Your Majesty," answered a man, either Montgomery or Chambers. He didn't sound overly enthusiastic, but the two men left the others to wait. The rain continued as the gray light disappeared.

Patrick felt his lip where Wilkinson had hit him. He wondered how they would find their way in the darkness, along the flooded banks and marshes—what the Old Man called billabongs.

Why did Wilkinson hit me? Patrick wondered, trying to sort out what had happened to them in the past few hours. He buried his face in his leaf bed and listened to some of the men talking.

"I understand it's only fifteen miles back to Echuca from Boomerang Bend," the prince told one of the others in a soft voice. "But there is no moon tonight. We can hardly see our hands in front of our faces. There's naught to do but wait for morning light."

"What about the sick man?" asked someone.

"He's resting. Better he sleeps, I should say."

"But where did he come from? He wasn't on board when we left Echuca."

"I agree it's curious," replied the prince. "But he seems to be some relation to the captain. We'll find out more in the morning."

Patrick wasn't so sure they should wait that long, but the prince was right about one thing: Patrick's father *was* sleeping.

"Pa?" Patrick whispered into the darkness beside him, just to make sure. He could hear his father's uneven, rasping breaths and the soft, feverish moans, but nothing that sounded like an answer back.

Father in heaven, Patrick finally found himself praying, *please help Pa to get better. And . . .*

He wasn't sure how to finish, or what he could ask for his father, except for what was obviously impossible. It seemed almost crazy, but he kept his eyes closed and gave up trying to think how hopeless it sounded.

And, Father, I ask that somehow—I don't know how, but somehow—if you would just step in and make it so Pa won't have to go back to jail.

The rain found a way through the leaves overhead, and he shivered.

Somehow . . .

Patrick lay curled up in a ball for what seemed like hours after the men had finally gone to sleep. He tried to get more comfortable as he listened to the dripping of the rain, to his father struggling for breath. In the distance he could hear the sounds of animals, sometimes the screech of a bat, he thought, or maybe an owl. Then he heard something else.

The terrible sound made the hair on the back of his neck stand straight up, and Patrick tried to remember where he had heard it before. He strained his ears; it was definitely moving closer.

"There it is again," he whispered to himself. The same low, husky snarl he had heard when the circus barge had lost its cargo by the Echuca wharf.

A tiger!

"Becky, wake up." Patrick crawled over to where he thought she was sleeping, but he couldn't quite see in the dark. "Becky?"

"Over here, Patrick" came a voice from behind him.

Patrick stumbled back to where Becky was sitting, waking a couple of people in the process.

"What are you doing?" she asked him. "Haven't you been asleep?"

"Too much noise. Did you hear the tiger?"

"Oh, Patrick. Let's not let our imaginations get away with us."

Patrick heard the growl again in the distance, and he grabbed his sister's arm. "There. Did you hear it this time?" he asked, and they were both still.

"I think you just heard thunder. Go back to sleep."

"But it wasn't thunder. It was the escaped circus tiger. I'm sure of it."

One of the other people cleared his throat. "I say, boy, would you keep it quiet over there?"

But by that time Patrick was determined.

"I'm going to wake up Pa," he decided, and Becky grabbed his arm.

"You are *not*!"

"Becky, you don't understand." He tried to pull away, but she dug her fingernails deep into his arm.

"Ow, Becky. Let me go!" Feeling hot anger in his cheeks, he pulled as hard as he could, and they fell to the ground.

"Patrick," protested his sister, "I can't believe you're—"

"What on earth?" The Old Man crawled up to where they were struggling and clamped his own strong hand over Patrick's shoulder. "People are trying to get some rest, and you two are fighting!"

"We're not fighting," Becky tried to explain. "Patrick said he was going to wake Pa. I was just trying to stop him."

"But I heard the tiger!" Patrick insisted as he tried to wriggle free of the Old Man. It was no use.

"He's just hearing things," hissed Becky, "and waking everyone up. He's acting . . . like a twelve-year-old."

"I *am* twelve."

"Exactly my point."

"You're not my mother. You can't order me—"

"Shh!" the Old Man cut him off. "That's enough, now."

"But the tiger," Patrick tried once more. "I heard it."

"Sure, and I heard thunder," countered his sister. "You're just dreaming."

"Tiger, eh?" The Old Man paused for a moment.

"She won't believe me," continued Patrick. "But just listen for a minute and you'll hear it, too."

The camp fell silent except for the night sounds, the dripping, and then the faint sound of distant thunder.

"There," said Becky. "Hear it? The great tiger."

"But that wasn't what I heard. Why won't you believe me, Becky?"

Becky sighed, and they waited another minute. It thundered again.

"All right, now," whispered the Old Man. "I've heard enough."

"But—"

"I don't want to hear any more noise from either of you. We have a bit of a walk in the morning, and we may have to carry your father."

Patrick's father was still wheezing, sleeping through all the noise. Becky settled back into her place. Patrick shivered and wished for a blanket.

"I know I heard the tiger," whispered Patrick.

"Thunder," she whispered back.

"Tiger."

"Thunder."

Another clap of thunder sounded in the distance. Patrick frowned and tried to find his spot in the leaves again.

Maybe it really was thunder, he thought, settling back down. But, no. He knew what he had heard, and he knew it wasn't the same. He strained his ears, and his eyes wouldn't close. Every shadow became a tiger in his imagination. The owl sounded like a tiger. The rain sounded like a tiger. Even his father's groaning sounded like a tiger, and Patrick wondered if he would recognize the real thing if he heard it again. He dozed, but restlessly.

The next time he heard thunder, it was straight overhead, and the flash of lightning woke him as much as the crash that followed on its heels. In the blue-white light he saw nearly everyone in the camp sitting up, their eyes wide with fright. Only his father kept his head down, though he rolled over. The rain had finally eased off, but his father looked as if he was drenched in feverish sweat.

"Pa." Becky crawled over and touched her father's forehead with the back of her hand, then wrinkled her own face in worry and looked at her brother. "He's still burn—"

The thunder crashed around them as if it would topple the tall eucalyptus trees on their heads. With their father between them, Patrick forgot about the tiger for a moment.

"We can't wait anymore," Patrick told his sister between flashes. "We need to get him to a doctor right away."

Becky nodded uncertainly and mopped at her father's forehead with a corner of her skirt.

Patrick was used to counting the seconds between a flash of lightning and the clap of distant thunder. This time there was no wait, and he felt a strange tingling in the air. And there was an awful burnt smell, like hot metal.

"Lightning strike!" announced the Old Man, and when Patrick

looked up in the canopy of trees above them, he heard the cracking of a branch peeling away from its trunk with a twisting screech. Almost instinctively, he grabbed for the Old Man, and they both ducked as a huge branch thundered to the ground only a few yards from where they stood.

Something screamed, and for a moment Patrick thought it sounded like a woman. But then he heard it again, this time only a few feet away.

"I heard it, too, this time, Patrick," said the Old Man, and he moved swiftly to pick up the largest stick he could find on the forest floor.

"Everyone gather closer," he said. "Over here!"

Patrick looked down at his father, who didn't move, and wished there were something more he could do to help him. The thunder and lightning hit again somewhere close by. In the odd flashes of light, they looked almost as if they were moving in slow motion.

"Grab a stick," the Old Man told them between claps of thunder, but Patrick was already stripping the branches off the longest one he could find. The thunder and lightning moved off swiftly without bringing any rain, and then they all heard it—the loudest, longest growl yet.

Now they'll believe me, thought Patrick.

They huddled close to his father, who was still lying on the ground with his eyes closed. Patrick imagined the giant cat leaping out of the bush, fangs flashing, just like the picture on the circus poster. No one had to explain what they were hearing this time.

"Don't say it, Patrick," whispered Becky, holding out her own stick.

"What do lions eat?" asked Prentice.

"Tiger," Patrick corrected him. "That's a tiger out there."

"They eat meat," added someone else. "It's probably hungry."

"We came all the way to Australia for this?" wondered another man. "What happened to the friendly little kangaroos?"

Everyone stopped complaining when they heard a rustling in

the bushes. Patrick's heart raced as he raised his stick and got ready to yell.

"No matter what, Becky," Patrick whispered hoarsely, "I'm not going to let that animal touch Pa."

CHAPTER 18

DANGER IN EVERY STEP

"I say, what's this?" asked a voice from the bushes. In a flash of lightning, Patrick saw Wilkinson, staring at the group, followed by Montgomery and Chambers. All three were completely drenched, their clothes covered with mud and their hair pasted to their heads.

"Is that you, Wilkinson?" ventured the prince, lowering his stick for a moment and leaning forward into the darkness. "You gave us a terrible fright."

Wilkinson cleared his throat and stepped closer.

"Dreadfully sorry," stammered Wilkinson. "Although you needn't have worried. I was quite all right down the river a ways once I was able to stand up. Then Montgomery and Chambers found me and—"

"Listen, that's enough of this chatter," interrupted the Old Man. "We've got a man here who needs a doctor's attention. Did you hear—"

"Did you hear the tiger?" Becky finished the sentence.

Wilkinson started laughing. "Forgive me, I thought you just said 'tiger.'"

The Old Man hit his stick against the palm of his hand. "That's exactly what she said."

"Oh dear, I seem to have left my notebook on your ship, but I recall having written in it that while Australia is home to a wide

129

variety of animals, there are no tigers here."

"I don't need a zoological lesson just now!" thundered the Old Man. "What I do need is for everyone to line up with their sticks, single file, and we'll make our way out of here. I'll go first and carry Johnny."

"Back the way I came?" sputtered Wilkinson, his voice trailing off. "Tigers?"

The Old Man only grunted as he picked up his son and hoisted him to his back, the same way a farmer would pick up a sack of heavy potatoes.

"Hold on, son," the Old Man whispered back to Mr. McWaid, and the feverish man weakly wrapped his arms around the Old Man's shoulders and neck before he whispered something.

"Nothing to be sorry for," the Old Man grunted as he adjusted his load and started marching. "Not your fault."

A weak flash of lightning lit up Patrick, standing next to the bewildered Wilkinson.

"Oh, it's you, my boy." Wilkinson acted as if he was glad to see Patrick again. He leaned closer to Patrick's ear before Patrick could pull away.

"We'll just forget that little episode on your grandfather's boat, won't we?" he asked in a low voice as they started walking.

"Episode?" replied Patrick. "Do you want me to forget that you hit me in the mouth?"

Wilkinson nervously cleared his throat. "Regrettable," he answered. "I'm truly sorry."

Patrick sighed, remembering the panic everyone on the boat had felt. The panic *he* had felt, too. Wilkinson had been scared—he knew that. And Patrick's lip was still sore, but . . .

"It's all right," he finally replied, just as the tiger growled again in the distance.

"What was that?" yelped Wilkinson, jumping nearly a foot into the air.

"Get a stick, man," ordered the Old Man, stumbling under the weight of his son. "As long and as stout as you can carry. That was your nonexistent tiger."

They had only stumbled a short distance before their trail—if that's what it was—led them back to the riverbank. Patrick could feel the spongy ground grab at his shoes even before they met the water, and he could smell the thick, damp air hovering above the stream. Raindrops hissed on the black surface of the widened, flooded Murray.

"There it is," said Becky, her voice quiet as if she were at a funeral. And perhaps they were; Patrick could barely make out the ghostly white outline of the wounded *Lady Elisabeth*, still wedged in place and mostly buried under thick, dark river water.

The prince broke the silence. "I do trust we'll be able to salvage your vessel, Captain."

"Aye." The Old Man looked at his ship blankly but said nothing else as they turned away from the river and Boomerang Bend. Patrick could hear the squishing sound of the mud as they struggled through the darkness.

They stumbled in single file through the dark, dripping forest, sometimes sinking up to their ankles in mud, sometimes catching a faint glimpse of the black river to their left. Patrick tried his best not to step on his sister's heels as he held his stick first out to the left, then to the right, jabbing it into the bushes as they went by.

"Stay away!" he said softly, hoping the tiger was too far away to hear anything they said. He tried to quicken his step to keep from shaking in the cold.

Is it following us?

Wilkinson, meanwhile, never stopped talking.

"Kangaroos I thought we'd see, and certainly a koala bear or two," the prince's aide told anyone who would listen. "Perhaps even that odd duck-billed creature. But *tigers*? If we'd been interested in tigers, I'm sure we could have visited the jungles of Sumatra instead. This is *Australia*, for goodness' sake. Am I to understand this animal is escaped from the circus?"

"Be glad you haven't run into any snakes yet," muttered the Old Man.

Patrick shivered at the thought and kept walking until the mud gripped at his foot and wouldn't let go. He paused and bent down to tug at his shoe, but in the half dark of the early morning, no one noticed he had fallen behind. With a giant sucking sound, he finally rescued his shoe and plugged it back on his foot.

"Wait a minute, Becky." He looked up for his sister—and saw a huge white tiger standing in his way, staring straight at him.

CHAPTER 19

DREAMING OR DEAD

Patrick couldn't speak, couldn't move, couldn't breathe. He wasn't sure, but he thought for a moment his heart might have stopped until he felt it pounding in his ears.

I'm dreaming—or I'm dead, he told himself. The tiger still eyed him with its cold, steady gaze. The animal bared its teeth and hissed.

"I hope you're not hungry," Patrick finally whispered. Without moving his feet, he reached slowly for his stick, hoping someone would notice he had lagged behind. The tiger took a careful step toward him and hissed once more.

"Go away," Patrick croaked, and the forest around him seemed to fall silent in the first morning light. Even the cat's big paws made no sound on the leaves as it approached Patrick, who stood like a statue with his stick raised. "Did you hear me? Get down!"

Patrick didn't know why he said that; somehow it made sense to order the sofa-sized white animal to get down.

"I said down!" he repeated. "GET DOWN!"

Obediently, the white tiger rolled over on its back, putting all four paws in the air and opening its mouth wide with a mighty hiss. Except for the two top teeth, which Patrick had seen before, all the other teeth were missing.

"Patrick?" Becky yelled from ahead, and Patrick heard his sister crashing back to find him. "Patrick, where did you go?"

Patrick didn't move a muscle, couldn't move, even with the tiger at his feet. He just stood guard with his stick raised over his head, breathing hard.

"Stay DOWN!" Patrick ordered the cat.

"Patrick?" Becky stopped short a few feet away when she spotted the tiger. "Oh no!" she gasped, rocking back on her tiptoes.

"So far it hasn't done anything except roll over on its back," reported Patrick. "Maybe it thinks this is the circus."

Becky swallowed hard and nodded. "Patrick, don't move. Don't run."

"Don't worry," replied Patrick. "I couldn't run if I wanted to."

Now what do I do? Patrick looked at the tiger's pink underside. *Scratch it on the belly?*

He noticed the cat still wore a thick red leather collar, trailing a frayed length of rope about ten feet long. The cat rolled over once more, hissed again, and swatted with its giant paw.

"I think it wants me to scratch it or something," said Patrick.

"It's a wild animal, Patrick," said Becky. "Don't do anything. Just back up slowly."

Someone else appeared behind Becky, catching the cat's attention. Suddenly it sprang up.

"Oh!" It was the prince, and he backed up in wide-eyed fright when he saw the large animal, just as Becky had done. The cat lowered, as if it would spring again.

"No, you don't." Patrick didn't think, he just grabbed at the tiger's leash and dug his heels in as if it were a runaway horse.

"Sit down!" he ordered in his gruffest voice, giving the collar a mighty yank.

The tiger gagged but sat, and Patrick found himself almost nose to nose with the white tiger, an animal at least three times his size. The tiger growled and swatted at him with a huge paw, just missing his shoulder as Patrick rolled to the side.

"Down!" yelled the prince, who held out his stick like a spear. He kept Becky behind him, and by that time the others had arrived to see what all the noise was about.

"What in the world?" cried the Old Man, pushing his way past the others. "Patrick! What on earth are you doing? Tie the rope to something and get out of there!"

Patrick desperately looked for something, anything that looked strong enough to tie the rope to. There were several trees around them, but none close enough. Only a sapling as thick as his arm. It would have to do.

"Hurry and tie it!" Becky urged him, but his fingers fumbled with the rope. The cat looked at them uncertainly, then back at Patrick, as if it were trying to decide who might taste better. The Old Man waved his stick over his head to attract the animal's attention.

"I've heard about white tigers," whispered Prince Alfred, "but I've never personally seen one. Oh, but wouldn't my hunting rifle be useful right now."

"I think it's as hungry as I am," explained Patrick, giving the leash a tug after he had tied five knots to attach the rope to the sapling. The tiger shook its head and looked at them.

"No doubt," said the prince. "This animal surely doesn't know how to hunt."

"Or chew," added Becky, looking closer at the big animal's mouth. "No teeth. And it looks pretty old and wrinkled."

The Old Man pulled his granddaughter back. "Old or not, this is no pet. Now, Patrick, come around slowly and join us."

Patrick tested the rope once more, frowned, and backed away. "This tree is not going to—"

A steam whistle echoed from the direction of the river.

"Someone's looking for us!" said Wilkinson, his face brightening.

"Yes, and it's about time, I'd say." Prince Alfred took the Old Man by the arm and dragged him toward the riverbank to meet the boat.

"Halloo!" cried Wilkinson, waving his arms and hurrying toward the riverbank. "We're over here! Halloo!"

The Old Man looked back. "Come along, Patrick. The circus

people can come back to claim their animal. We'll tell them where to find it."

Everyone else hurried for the river, leaving Becky, Patrick, and the tiger.

"Why does it keep sniffing at me?" asked Patrick, trying to keep his distance. He felt at his back pocket, where he discovered a soft package wrapped in a cloth napkin.

"Oh no," he groaned. "I forgot all about this."

Patrick held up a completely flattened roast beef sandwich, the one he had saved from Becky's food tray the day before.

Becky groaned. "That's horrible, Patrick. I can't believe you just put something like that in your pocket and forgot it."

Another blast of the whistle echoed up and down the river, and through the trees in the early dawn Patrick could make out a puff of smoke as an open steam launch nosed in to shore. Wilkinson was the first to help pull in the boat; Patrick recognized the square red-and-white-striped canopy with the fringe hung around the steam engine and the short black smokestack in the middle.

One of the smaller boats from Echuca, thought Patrick.

"I don't know the fellow in front," Becky told her brother, "but look who just stood up in back."

Patrick squinted, and his blood ran cold.

"Becky." He pulled back behind a couple of trees. "That's Conrad Burke!"

CHAPTER 20

NOT AGAIN!

"What is *he* doing here?" whispered Becky, finding shelter behind a fallen log.

"I don't know." Patrick gritted his teeth. "But it looks as if Grandpa just realized who it is, too."

They watched helplessly as their grandfather took a step backward from the river, still carrying their father. Burke reached into his coat to pull out a shiny gray revolver, and they heard Wilkinson gasp.

"Hear, now, there's no need for that revolver." Prince Alfred stood next to the Old Man. "There must be some mistake."

Burke didn't lower the pistol he held in his hand. With his free hand, he handed the prince what looked like a poster.

"I'm sorry, Your Majesty, there's no mistake. Are you denying this is the same John McWaid described here in this newspaper?"

The Old Man lowered his son gently to the ground, then held him around the shoulders to keep him from falling. Patrick couldn't hear what he said to the prince.

"You see, Your Majesty?" crowed Burke. "He even admits it. This man here is an escaped convict. An outlaw with a price on his head."

The prince's friends backed away from where the Old Man and Mr. McWaid were standing.

"Yes, that's right," continued Burke. "I came to protect you, and I'll be taking John McWaid back with me to the authorities now."

"You!" exploded the Old Man, pointing his finger at Burke. "You had no intention of protecting the prince. Why, *you're* the one the authorities actually want."

"Me?" sputtered Burke in pretend surprise.

"That's right," continued the Old Man. "Johnny never hurt anyone. Sure but I could tell the authorities a story or two about you, and so could my grandchildren."

Burke pointed the long-nosed revolver in the Old Man's face for effect. "My dear Captain, I'm afraid you must have me confused with someone else. And I obviously have never had the pleasure of meeting your grandchildren."

"He's lying, Your Majesty," fumed the Old Man.

"Captain, Captain. Let me remind you that you are aiding an outlaw, are you not? That's illegal. Now, you wouldn't want to get hurt, as well. . . ."

"I'll not bow to your threats, Mr. Burke. Not now and not ever."

Mr. McWaid broke away from his father's supporting arms. "No, Father. I'll go with him. I don't want anyone to get hurt."

Patrick could hardly believe what he was watching. His father took an unsteady step away from the Old Man.

"Smart man, McWaid." Burke chuckled. "You know when to cooperate, don't you? Now, let's just get you into the boat and be on our way."

"You mean to say you're not willing to transport Prince Alfred?" interrupted Wilkinson, who was standing behind the prince.

"There is nothing I would rather do," answered Burke, not looking back, "but it is simply too dangerous to allow His Majesty in the same boat with this treacherous criminal. Most undignified, as well, wouldn't you say? I'll send for another more suitable vessel the moment we arrive back in Echuca."

Patrick looked at his sister for help. "We can't just sit here. Burke isn't taking Pa to the authorities. No one will ever see him again."

Becky nodded her head in agreement.

A sudden snapping sound came from behind. Patrick glanced back just in time to see the tiger come bounding in their direction.

"The tiger!" he said, grabbing his sister by the arm and running toward the water.

Burke was just pulling Mr. McWaid onto the launch. Everyone looked up when they heard Patrick yelling, and Patrick guessed by the looks on their faces that the big cat was probably a step behind him, ready to pounce.

"Into the boat!" shouted Patrick.

"What?" Burke looked as the small crowd parted to either side.

Just a few more steps to the boat, Patrick thought wildly, *then jump at Burke*. He remembered his sandwich in his free hand and threw it behind him.

Panic-stricken, Burke dropped Mr. McWaid like a stone and fired off a couple of wild shots over their heads. Still Patrick and Becky ran, arms waving wildly and screaming like wild animals.

"Stop him, Becky!" Patrick called to his sister.

Burke leveled his aim straight at the tiger, but Patrick's father grabbed his leg and they both tumbled onto the deck. Patrick and Becky arrived just in time to each hold an arm, but it was clear right away they wouldn't be able to hold on. With the gun waving in his face, Patrick did the only thing he could think of—he bit into the back of the man's hand.

Burke howled in pain, and the gun clattered onto the floorboards of the river launch. With the Old Man's help, they wrestled Burke to the bottom of the boat. The man who had come with Burke was hiding behind the steam engine, which was still hissing. Almost everyone else had jumped into the river—only a couple had run down the short beach in terror.

The tiger, meanwhile, had stopped to examine Patrick's sandwich, and it licked its lips for more, sniffing its way around the beach.

Dripping wet himself, Prince Alfred gingerly picked up the gun and handed it to Wilkinson. He then helped Mr. McWaid into the boat while Burke squirmed and grumbled on the floorboards.

"You fools!" complained Burke, arching his back. "Why didn't you let me shoot it?"

"No need," the Old Man replied quietly. "You're slightly more dangerous to us at the moment."

"No need?" howled Burke. "You must be mad."

"Mad." The Old Man chuckled. "That's almost amusing, coming from you."

Becky and Patrick helped the others aboard the launch; most of them kept as far away from the beach and the pacing tiger as they could.

"I have a right to capture an escaped prisoner!" howled Burke, but the Old Man had a firm lock on his arms from behind. "And I will not be made to look like a fool."

"Well, but you're too late for that, Mr. Burke," replied the Old Man, forcing Burke to the floor. "But you remind me of an old Irish saying."

"What are you babbling about?"

"My father used to tell me, 'Everyone is wise until he speaks.' In your case, Mr. Burke, you would have done much better had you kept your mouth shut."

"I insist that you release me!" Burke squirmed, but the Old Man only held him more tightly.

"Now, wait." The prince held up his hands. "I'm sure we can solve this. . . ."

"Aye, without further ado," finished the Old Man. "Patrick, why don't you check our friend's pockets, here, just to make sure he's not carrying any more weapons. Will you do that, please?"

Patrick hesitated, but the Old Man nodded at him, so he reached down and checked Burke's vest pockets, shirt pocket, and the pockets of Burke's finely tailored slacks.

"You won't find anything." Burke practically spit at Patrick.

"There's a gold watch and a handkerchief," Patrick reported back, "but no gun."

"Good." The Old Man nodded and eased up. "Now, make sure your pa is comfortable, will you, and we'll see about getting him to a doctor."

While the others climbed aboard, Becky crouched over the slumped form of their father in the corner of the boat. She looked back at them, her forehead wrinkled with concern.

The Old Man turned to the man who had been hiding behind the steam engine—the man who had been running the boat. "Let's be on our way quickly, then, shall we, George?"

George nodded and made himself busy fiddling with the valves and controls of his steam engine. He was nearly toothless, stooped, and much older than even the Old Man. By the way it hissed and sputtered, his steam engine was older yet.

"Nobody told me anything about tigers or convicts," muttered George. A large wheel started turning on the side of his engine, slowly at first, then with more noise and power as they backed into the middle of the river. Something clanked inside the engine as steam and woodsmoke huffed out the little stack. "This man just told me we had to go pick up someone a few miles upstream. I didn't even know who he was."

"And you didn't ask, right, George?" The Old Man looked down at Burke, who was sitting on the floorboards. "Just a Sunday morning excursion. And I suppose he probably paid you in advance."

"Even so, I'm glad you happened along," said Prince Alfred brightly.

The Old Man frowned and raised his voice over the huffing and clanking of the steam engine. "I assure you he didn't happen along, Your Majesty. Mr. Burke intended to find us, or rather, he intended to track down my son by stopping our paddle steamer if necessary."

"Yes, well." The prince glanced with a worried expression at the edge of the overloaded river launch. "I'm sure the authorities will be able to help us sort out this misunderstanding, one way or another. And at this rate, we'll be back in Echuca before noon. Surely no one has any objections to *that*?"

The Old Man sighed and looked at Mr. McWaid. "He needs a doctor."

Burke said nothing, only glared at Wilkinson, who was still fumbling nervously with the gun. The captured man's dark expression sent a chill up Patrick's spine.

CHAPTER 21

UNFRIENDLY HELLO

"There's the wharf." Patrick tapped his sister impatiently on the shoulder as they approached Echuca. "I thought we'd never make it."

George frowned as if to say it wasn't his fault they had run out of wood and had to go ashore to chop more. And Patrick knew it wouldn't do any good to complain about the three times they'd had to stop while George repaired his ancient steam engine. At least they had made it . . . almost. The engine wheezed to a stop yet again.

"How's your pa?" asked the Old Man.

Becky shook her head. "Worse than before, I think. He was talking for a while, but he's shaking again."

"I'll run to get the doctor as soon as we tie up," volunteered Patrick.

Prince Alfred cleared his throat as the boat drifted closer. "I must ask, Mr. Burke, that you stay aboard until we locate the constable. Of course, if your story checks out and with the permission of the local authorities, my aide will be happy to return your revolver."

Burke shrugged. "Why not? I certainly have nothing to hide."

His eyes narrowed, however, when he looked at what was going on at the wharf. Several people were pointing at them.

"What's happening on the wharf, Grandpa?" asked Becky, looking concerned. "All those people aren't unloading paddle steamers."

It's almost dinnertime, so they haven't just been to church. Patrick could see the crowd, too. As they drew closer he could see that several of the men carried long shotguns. A minute later they were close enough to hear someone shout.

"If you don't live here," yelled the man on the edge of the wharf, "keep going!"

They didn't have to answer; by that time someone else recognized them.

"It's George!" Patrick heard someone say. "And he's got Prince Alfred with him!"

The wharf erupted into even more panic as several of the men ran into town. The prince looked nervously at their greeting party.

"What's happening, Captain?" he asked the Old Man, who could only shake his head.

"We'll find out in a minute."

Patrick got ready to throw them a line, and they glided expertly to a stop between two larger paddle steamers.

"Get your boat secured right away," shouted one of the men. It was Constable Fitzgerald, though he wasn't wearing his usual formal constable's helmet. "We'll escort you to the church if you don't have a home nearby. And, Your Highness, we'll of course take you directly to your hotel."

"But what—" began the Old Man.

"There's at least one tiger loose in the town." The constable checked his weapon before going on. "Maybe two, and we've heard reports from all over."

Patrick's father was now sitting up, though pale and barely conscious.

"My father!" Patrick told the men on the dock. "He's sick. We have to get him to a doctor."

Constable Fitzgerald looked suspiciously into the boat, then frowned and motioned for another man to come.

"Where did you find this man?"

"It's a long story," answered the Old Man. "He's—"

"Do you realize who this is?" The constable brought his shotgun around and pointed it squarely at Mr. McWaid, who didn't open his eyes. Becky and Patrick didn't leave their father's side.

"For heaven's sake, put the gun down, Alexander," answered the Old Man. "Of course I know who this is. But as you can see—"

"Mitchell!" Constable Fitzgerald shouted. "Get down here. We have a prisoner! I believe this is John McWaid."

The Old Man ran his hand impatiently through his silver hair and stepped in front of his son. "We have a *patient*. He needs a doctor. Probably doesn't even hear what we're saying, he's so feverish."

The constable looked up for just a moment, studying the Old Man's face. Finally, slowly, he lowered his gun. "How do I know this isn't some sort of ruse? A trick?"

The Old Man stepped over and lifted his son up by the shoulders. "Use your sense for just a moment, Alexander. Would he come *here* if it was a trick? This man needs to see a doctor, and soon!"

The man in charge frowned. "Mitchell, you'd better help drag this fellow up to see Doc Thompson. I want you to stay on guard there, though, until I send someone to replace you. Can he walk?"

Patrick shook his head no.

"All right, then," said the constable, turning toward town. "I'll inform the doctor you'll be there shortly."

In a minute they had dragged Mr. McWaid out of the boat and up to the wharf. The Old Man pointed at Patrick.

"You go with him, boy. I'll take Becky and fetch your mother at the cabin. We'll meet you back at the clinic."

Patrick looked down at the boat, empty by that time except for the Old Man, George the boatman, and Wilkinson, who was still holding Burke's gun. Something wasn't right.

Wait a minute, Patrick's heart sank. *What happened to. . . ?*

"Grandpa! Burke is gone!"

The Old Man turned on Wilkinson, who had been watching the unloading of Mr. McWaid like everyone else. The gun in his hand pointed harmlessly down at the river.

"What happened to him?" demanded the Old Man.

Wilkinson looked around, as if he had just awakened from a nap. "He was right here. . . ."

"Ahh, come now." The Old Man stomped his foot in disgust. "You just let him slip over the side and swim away, did you? Here, give me that gun."

Looking as if he was afraid the Old Man would hit him, Wilkinson handed the pistol across and hurried for the ladder to the wharf.

"I'm terribly, terribly sorry, but I must be off. You see, His Majesty will be needing me, and . . ."

"Go on." The Old Man waved him off, then turned to look at his grandson. "Don't pay it any mind, Patrick. I don't expect we'll ever see Mr. Burke again. Now, go see to your father."

Patrick did as he was told, picking up his father by the legs while Mitchell took hold under his arms.

"Doesn't someone have a stretcher?" Patrick asked.

Mitchell didn't answer as they hobbled up the deserted Hare Street toward a storefront clinic.

"Where is everyone?" he asked.

Mitchell sweated, struggling with the weight of Patrick's father. "Everyone's been ordered off the street, with the tiger sightings."

"Safe to come out yet, Constable?" someone shouted from a doorway.

Patrick noticed curious, fearful faces staring at them through shop windows, through the windows above stores.

"Constable Fitzgerald will give you the word," the man grunted back without looking up. "Just stay where you are."

A few more steps down the muddy road, Mitchell pointed to a storefront with his chin. A man Patrick guessed was the doctor met them at the door.

"Inside, quickly!" barked the doctor, a middle-aged man with long sideburns that almost formed a beard, but not quite. He looked nervously up and down the street. "Constable Fitzgerald told me you were on your way."

They laid Mr. McWaid on a bed in the second back room. It was plainly furnished, and clear jars of strange liquids were stacked in cabinets that lined the wall. The smells almost made Patrick sick. Medicine smells, he supposed, but he wondered how the things in the doctor's office would make his father well.

"How long has he been like this?" asked the doctor, listening to Mr. McWaid's raspy breathing through a flexible tube pressed to his chest. The constable retreated to the main room to check out the window and stand by the front door, his arms crossed.

"With a fever?" answered Patrick. "We're not sure. But he started getting worse just last night. He's been really hot."

The doctor nodded as he poked and prodded his patient's chest. "Fevers, then chills?"

Patrick nodded.

"And very weak, can't stand up?" Dr. Thompson pushed gently under Mr. McWaid's ribs, as if he was looking for something.

"We've had to carry him."

"Internal swelling," the doctor mumbled as he listened again through his stethoscope tube. He continued poking and prodding as he asked a few more questions about how Patrick's father had been feeling and acting and where he had been the past few months.

"Is he going to be all right?" Patrick finally asked.

The doctor shook his head. "Certainly not if you hadn't brought him in when you did."

"But he *is* going to be all right?"

"I can't say for certain yet, but my first impression is that your father has picked up a severe case of malaria, young man. Unusual, but possible, if he's been traveling about."

"People die from malaria?" Patrick thought even the name sounded life-threatening.

"People die, but we can treat it."

Patrick mopped his father's forehead with a damp cloth and nodded seriously.

"He also doesn't look as if he's eaten in quite a while," continued the doctor. "He's very weak. I'd like to keep him here for a couple of days, before . . ."

He glanced at the constable through the open door to the front room. The man didn't look as if he was paying particular attention as he gazed out the window. "Before the police take him off to prison again."

"My ma—I mean, my mother will be here soon," Patrick explained. "She hasn't seen him in a long time."

"She'll have plenty of time to visit. I don't think he's going anywhere for a while."

Patrick nodded again and helped the doctor prop his father up against a pillow.

"You're going to be fine, Pa," Patrick told him.

Mr. McWaid smiled back at them weakly as the doctor rolled up his sleeve.

"Hey, are we about done in there?" drawled the constable, stepping into the room. He frowned when the doctor told him about Mr. McWaid's condition.

"Constable Fitzgerald's not going to like this."

"Constable Fitzgerald doesn't have a choice," answered the doctor. He turned to a table and picked up a large, wicked-looking hypodermic needle.

"What's that?" asked Patrick.

"It's a new kind of treatment. Now, this is going to sting a little, Mr. McWaid, something like a bee-sting, if you've ever experienced that."

Patrick's father didn't seem to notice the shot, but the burly policeman turned white and quickly left the room. Patrick had to close his eyes. A minute later the doctor was leading him out of the room.

"Patrick!" whispered Mr. McWaid, holding up his hand. "Wait."

Patrick had to lean over to hear what his father was trying to tell him.

"I'm here, Pa."

Mr. McWaid swallowed hard. "Listen, son. If I don't . . ."

Tears welled up in Patrick's eyes. "Please don't say that, Pa. You're going to be all right."

Patrick's father shook his head, reached up, and gripped his son's shirt. "Listen, son. I'm very sick, but no matter what happens, I'll still be free. Jail can't change that. Not even death . . ."

"Please, Pa . . ."

"That verse keeps going around and around in my head, Patrick." His father swallowed hard. "All the way here, on the ship, hiding these past few months."

He was quiet a few moments, as if looking for the strength to finish.

" 'Neither death, nor life, nor angels . . . ' " He swallowed again. "You know the verse. Finish it."

Patrick knew, but he didn't want to finish. It sounded too much like "good-bye" to him. Still his father squeezed his hand, urging him on.

" 'Nor principalities, nor powers,' " Patrick took a deep breath, " 'nor things present, nor things to come, nor height, nor depth, nor any other creature . . . ' " He couldn't finish, just buried his face in his father's shoulder.

". . . 'shall be able to separate us from the love of God,' " Mr. McWaid gasped out the rest of the Bible verse, " 'which is in Christ Jesus our Lord.' "

Patrick cried into his father's shoulder.

"I understand, Pa." He rocked his forehead slowly, crying quietly, until his father's hand fell limply to the side.

The doctor stepped up to check Mr. McWaid's labored, shallow breathing, then gently pulled Patrick away.

"Let him rest, son," he whispered, leading him out of the room.

"That was quinine I gave him," Dr. Thompson explained when they were alone in the front room and the door was closed. "Quite potent. It should help with the fever, and we'll follow up with pills. But he may be in and out of consciousness for a while. Did you say your mother. . . ?"

Patrick nodded and wiped his eyes with the sleeve of his shirt. "She should be here pretty soon."

"Fine. I see our constable friend went down the street. Probably got hungry."

Without warning Patrick's own stomach rumbled, and the doctor chuckled.

"You're hungry yourself."

Patrick shook his head. "I'm fine. Starving, but fine."

"Oh, really? Well, so am I." He paused for only a second. "And they serve a great jumbuck stew down at the Shamrock."

"Sir?" Patrick wasn't sure why the doctor mentioned it, or what "jumbuck" was.

"Mutton stew, and quite tasty. So you just wait here, and I'll be right back with a couple of bowls. All right? Don't touch anything."

"Oh, I wouldn't." Patrick could hardly argue with the offer, so the doctor hurried out and down the street in the gathering dark.

By the light of a single oil lamp, Patrick could see the main examining room was decorated with framed pictures of skeletons, medical diagrams, and the doctor's certificates from medical school in England. Most of the walls were covered by glass cases lined with shelves filled with bottles of strange-looking powders and liquids. A large, heavy table filled the center of the room, covered by a blanket and near another cabinet filled with the doctor's equipment. Patrick wandered around the room, afraid to touch anything, when he heard a dull thud in the other room, then a crash of glass breaking on the floor.

"Pa?" Patrick called into the darkness. He wasn't expecting an answer, but he grabbed the lamp from the table and opened the door to find an empty bed. The sheets were thrown off wildly onto the floor.

He can't be gone! Patrick told himself, but it took only a quick look under and around the other side of the bed to see that he was. A bottle of quinine pills had shattered on the floor between the plain bed and the window, but everything in the room was still. Only the lacy curtains from the windows fluttered in the breeze from the back alley.

"Dr. Thompson!" cried Patrick, running back to the front room. "He's gone!"

CHAPTER 22

HIDING IN THE SHADOWS

Where did the doctor say he was going? Patrick tried to remember the name of the restaurant, but he wasn't sure. He could see no one else out on the street, either, including the constable. Then he remembered the tigers.

Now what? he asked himself, returning to the room where his father had been lying. He checked out the window, but it was getting too dark to see past the shadows. To the left, down a small lane, he thought he saw something move against the back of the building next door.

At least it doesn't look like a tiger, he told himself, vaulting outside and landing in the lane.

"Pa?" he called out softly. He tiptoed carefully toward the shadow, waiting for an answer, ready to spring back to the safety of the window. He listened for a growl but heard nothing. No one moved.

"Is that you, Pa?"

Patrick jumped when someone coughed. It didn't sound like his father.

I don't think it's Pa, Patrick decided, taking another step toward the shadow. *But maybe in his fever he doesn't know what he's doing. Like sleepwalking.*

When Patrick bent over to see better, he nearly bumped into

someone leaning against the back of the building, hiding in the shadows. It was obviously not a tiger, but not his father, either. He gasped when he saw the long hook nose and the unmistakable cross-eyed stare.

Sebastian Weatherby.

"Oh!" Patrick started to backtrack but stumbled over a bottle and fell on his back. He tried to get away, but Sebastian was too quick, and Patrick felt himself lifted by the front of the shirt to his feet.

"What are you doing out here, kid? Haven't you heard about the tigers?"

"I heard. So why are *you* out here? Didn't your parents—"

Patrick stopped himself when he remembered that Sebastian Weatherby had no parents. Sebastian shrugged and let go of Patrick's shirt.

"Just wanted to see for myself."

Maybe he saw something, thought Patrick.

"So did you see anybody coming out that window over there?" Patrick pointed at the back of the clinic.

"What if I did?"

Patrick sighed. "Please, I don't have time to play games. I know you hate me. But you have to tell me what you saw. Please. Did you or did you not see someone coming out that window over there?"

Sebastian laughed softly. "All right. So why are you looking for the two men who came out of that window?"

Patrick swallowed hard. "Two? You saw two?"

"That's what I'm telling you, Irish boy. I was just on my way down this street, see, and I heard something, so I hid back here. And then out of the window they come, one half dead, the other one with his arm around the fellow's neck, saying they're going to go for a little swim. Didn't recognize either of them."

Patrick sighed in disbelief. "So Burke came back!"

"Burke? Who's that?"

"Don't have time to explain." Patrick jerked to life, kicking the bottle out of his way. Tigers or no tigers, he had to catch up with them. "My pa's the half-dead one. Which way did they go?"

Sebastian leaned out of the shadow enough to look down the lane, back toward the river and the Peninsula.

"Thanks, Sebastian," he called over his shoulder as he ran down the lane. A moment later something exploded behind him. A pop, and then he heard—almost felt—something graze his ear. Something like a rock—or a bullet.

"Hold it there!" yelled someone from behind him. "Or I won't miss next time!"

Patrick's legs wouldn't stop moving. All he could think to do was dive to the left, behind a garbage bin. It smelled as if something had either died in the bin, or the dog scraps were well aged. Another shot echoed behind the buildings and slammed into the mud at his feet.

"I said stop!" yelled the man, and then Patrick recognized Constable Mitchell's voice.

"It's just me!" Patrick yelled back, his knees knocking together. He thought of putting out his hand in a wave of surrender but decided against it. In a moment the constable was standing in front of him, his pistol pointed at Patrick's nose.

"*What* is going on here?" demanded the man, catching his breath. "Where is—"

"I heard a noise and went back to check the room," explained Patrick, still not sure how safe it would be to come out from behind the garbage. "And my father was gone."

"I noticed that. For a moment I thought you were him."

Patrick hesitated for a moment, wondering if he should repeat the part Sebastian had told him, about the second man.

"I *knew* it was all an act," snorted the constable as Patrick scrambled to his feet. "The prisoner plays dead so he can escape from the clinic. I've heard about that sort of thing before. Just not here in Echuca."

"But that's not what happened," said Patrick, dusting off his pants and standing up. "You don't understand."

"I understand enough to know that my prisoner is gone," snapped the constable. "And it looks as if he runs pretty well for someone with—what was it the good doctor said . . . malaria?"

"He *is* sick," insisted Patrick. "Someone came and dragged him off."

The constable snorted. "Oh, come now. I thought you said he was gone when you entered the room. Now you say you saw him dragged off?"

"No . . . I . . . but I'm sure he was. . . ."

"Save your breath, lad, and get back inside. The tigers are still about, which your father will find out presently. Make my job a whole lot easier."

"How can you say that?" Patrick didn't know what to say anymore, but his feet still wanted to run.

"Patrick?" The doctor was standing by the front of the clinic, looking their way, a small lantern hanging from his teeth and a bowl in each hand.

"Dr. Thompson!" Patrick ran toward the man. "Someone's taken my father!"

"What he means is that the bloke ran off," added the constable. "The way I see it, he had you pretty well fooled, didn't he, doctor?"

"I don't know what you're talking about." The doctor set the bowls down on the front step of the clinic and rushed inside, only to reappear a moment later. His eyes were wide, his face pale in the flickering yellow light of his lantern.

"What did I tell you?" asked the constable in a mocking tone.

"I can assure you, Constable, that man did not escape on his own two feet." The doctor looked up and down the street, and it started to rain again.

The constable checked his gun quickly and shook his head. "Doesn't matter either way. Now, go back in and keep your doors and windows shut."

"I'm going with you," insisted Patrick.

The constable shook his head. "No chance of that, lad. Get back inside."

"I'm sorry, sir." Patrick didn't blink. "But I know which way he went. A fellow out in back saw them. He told me."

"That so?" The constable snorted in laughter as he walked away.

"Wouldn't believe everything you hear. I'm checking the train station."

"But—"

The constable didn't stop, so Patrick ran off in the opposite way toward the Peninsula as an open wagon pulled by a single horse came hurrying down the street. He didn't look up to see who was driving until the wagon had almost run him down.

"Whoa!" yelled the driver, and Patrick recognized his grandfather's voice. He looked up in surprise to see his mother riding in the bench seat next to the Old Man and Becky. Michael bounced up on his hands and knees in the back end.

"Patrick!" His mother stood as the wagon skidded to a stop. "Patrick, whatever are you doing out here? Why aren't you still back at the clinic with your father?"

"Ma—"

"Well, never you mind, Patrick," his mother interrupted him with a smile as she waved a letter over her head. "Your father is free!"

For a moment Patrick was confused. *Free? How?*

"The letter, Patrick." His sister pointed to the letter their mother was waving. "Ma got it yesterday afternoon after we left. It tells everything. The police commissioner who had Pa put in jail was caught, and he confessed to accepting bribes right after we left Dublin. It's just taken this long for the news to catch up with us."

Patrick shook his head and pointed down the street. "No, you don't understand. Burke is—"

"Patrick, don't you see?" His mother stomped her feet in a little jig and put her arm around the Old Man. "Your pa is vindicated. He's free! We don't have to worry about Mr. Burke any longer."

"Yes, we do, Ma, because he just dragged Pa out the back window of the clinic and down toward the river!"

The Old Man's jaw dropped. "Well, what are we sitting here in the middle of the street for, young man? Get in the wagon!"

Patrick obeyed, and the Old Man wheeled the wagon around to race them back down the deserted street. The good news about the letter somehow didn't matter now.

"Sebastian saw them." Patrick crouched over his grandfather's shoulder as they flew down the street toward the Murray. "Said they went down this street. I think maybe he's going to throw him in the river, otherwise he would have already—"

The Old Man held up his hand to keep Patrick from finishing. Mrs. McWaid winced, as if someone had just hit her.

"I'm sorry, Ma," Patrick told her. "We have to stop Burke before something happens."

His mother looked at the Old Man, who whipped his reins to make the horse hurry. Patrick peered nervously into the dark street up ahead, which was lit only by the occasional lantern. At the end of the road, three or four men waved their lanterns for them to stop, but the Old Man only urged the horse on.

"Hey, now!" yelled one of the men with the lanterns. "Stop right there!"

"Out of the way!" roared the Old Man, waving his hand for them to move. Instead, one of the men raised a shotgun to his shoulder— and aimed it directly at them.

CHAPTER 23

CHASE THROUGH THE CIRCUS

"What do you think you're doing?" yelled one of the men.

Patrick thought he looked familiar; maybe he had seen him working at the circus. But their horse pulled up on its two rear legs, jolting the wagon so Patrick tumbled over the side to the dirt street below. Patrick yelped but then pressed himself to the ground.

"My son's been taken!" replied the Old Man as if that explained everything.

"Sorry, but no one is going past the end of the road," replied the man. "Not until we round up the tigers. Now, turn around and go home."

Now's my chance, thought Patrick, and he slithered backward on his stomach as quietly as he could, away from the wagon.

"Listen here—" The Old Man wasn't giving up, and then Patrick heard his mother say something. As the voices grew more and more urgent, Patrick got to his knees, then turned toward the river and ran blindly through the trees.

Where has he taken you, Pa? Patrick wanted to scream out into the night. As he sprinted toward the dark shapes of the quiet circus tents, his toe caught against a tent stake, and he flew into a canvas wall.

"Oh!" he cried, scrambling to his feet. Something growled long and low from the other side of the tent, and the hair on the back of Patrick's neck stood on end.

I've heard that before, he thought and considered running back the way he had come. But from somewhere behind him, he heard men shouting and making cracking noises with whips. He looked over his shoulder to see a line of lanterns as they lit up a dozen eerie faces.

Lord, please help me find Pa! he prayed. He had to make it to the river.

Backing away from the growling sound, he ran between two other tents, trying to remember how the circus had been set up. It seemed like a maze now.

This way?

He heard the snarl again and spun to see the outline of a very large tiger. Lanterns flickered in the distance behind the enormous cat. Patrick couldn't see its eyes, but he could feel them on him, and neither moved for a long moment.

"Stay," he croaked, his heart racing. "Down. Go away."

Patrick had the feeling *this* cat wasn't toothless. He backed up and tripped over another rope, then raced around the corner of another tent.

Why don't they catch it?

As the line of men came closer, Patrick ran away from them and the circus tents—straight for the river. He didn't dare turn around, but he was sure the tiger was following.

Up ahead, he could hear the patter of the steady rain on the river again. There was a shot from the far side of the tents, then a shout from the men, and Patrick looked back to see the lanterns bobbing wildly in between the tents, as if the men were running in circles.

"This way!" yelled one. Several more shots, and "I think I hit something!"

This must be what a war is like, Patrick told himself, stumbling down a low bank to the river's edge, then sinking to his knees in the cold black water. For a brief instant he saw the cat again, bounding his direction. Patrick crouched down in the water, praying silently and waiting for the tiger to flash by—but it never came.

The men's lanterns cast long shadows on the river. Some men sounded as though they carried frying pans that they banged with metal spoons to frighten the tiger in their hunt. Ahead of him something else splashed along the river.

Did the tiger run ahead of me? Patrick wondered, looking both ways. Someone grunted and there was a muffled cry ahead of him. Definitely not a tiger.

"Pa?" Patrick strained to see in the flickering shadows. He thought he saw two figures up ahead in the distance. He couldn't be sure, but as he ran, he heard more splashing behind him, more shouting, more shots. The men with the lanterns were much closer now. Patrick had the terrible feeling that the men were hunting *him*.

"Pa!" he cried. "Where are you?"

Where is he, God? he prayed desperately.

A few steps later Patrick could see Conrad Burke wrestling with someone in the water. It had to be Pa. As Burke turned for a moment, his face was framed in the light from someone's lantern—a grotesque mask of a face, wrinkled into a permanent, horrible frown. He looked around, and his sunken black eyes seemed fired with hate, a snake trapped in the light of a hunter.

Patrick never saw what hit him from behind, a heavy club of some sort that caught him just in back of the right ear. He gasped for breath, fighting the burning pain and the horrible clawing feeling of darkness—but everything closed in around him, and he couldn't move his arms or legs.

"Pa!" he cried in agony as he slipped into the blackness of the water. He struggled against the pain, against a heavy net that suddenly tangled him in its close grip.

CHAPTER 24

AWAY FROM THE MOB

Patrick almost blacked out, but he managed to roll over in the water, caught in a strong net the men had thrown on top of him. Someone stood over him, his club raised, while someone else pointed a lantern light in his face. Patrick couldn't even hold up his hands in defense. All he could do was shout.

"I'm not the tiger!" he screamed. "You're making a mistake! My pa! He was just pushed into the river, and he can't swim. . . . You have to help him!"

Patrick knew his father was normally a good swimmer, but not in his condition. Where was Burke?

And the tiger?

All Patrick could see was a confused mob of running men and bobbing lanterns. They seemed to be throwing their nets at anything that moved. But the tiger had disappeared, or at least Patrick couldn't see it anymore.

"Aw, it's just a kid," said the man with the club. "With all the splashing, I thought it was the cat."

He finally lowered his weapon. Patrick heard another splash, something struggling in the water. A groan. *Pa!*

"Hey, look there," said one of the hunters as Patrick finally wiggled free. The man with the club tried to grab him, but Patrick ducked away.

"Out there," said the other man, and a few of them trained their lights out over the water, just a few feet from the shore.

Patrick already knew what he was looking for; he lunged out into chest-deep water and grabbed his father's arm.

"Patrick," coughed the man, unable to stand. Patrick put his father's arm around his shoulder and pulled him to safety. Just beyond them, out in the river, one of the lanterns caught a glimmer of a pair of eyes. The tiger was swimming away!

A rifle went off above their heads, but Patrick didn't stop.

"Downstream!" someone yelled, but Patrick didn't care anymore about the tiger. He silently cheered for the escaping animal as the men turned away from them.

Swim for it, he urged the tiger as he and his father collapsed on the riverbank. He wasn't sure if anyone saw them in the confusion, but he could only gasp for breath as the sharp smoke of gunfire filled the air. He turned to his father.

"Pa? Can you hear me?" Patrick shook his father's shoulders gently, but they felt like Becky's rag doll. Mr. McWaid turned his head to look at Patrick and groaned.

"Come on, Pa, we've got to get you back to the clinic before Burke comes back."

Patrick tried to stand, tried to catch the attention of the man who had clubbed him on the head.

"Mister!" he cried, but the man was moving off with the rest of the mob, following the escaping tiger. The man turned back for a moment.

"Terribly sorry, boy. I don't know what you're doing here, but you'd best get home right now. And take your friend with you. It's dangerous out here."

"But we need help!" replied Patrick. The man disappeared into the darkness without another word.

"All right, Pa." Patrick sighed and tried to stand with the weight of his father draped around his shoulders, but he fell to his knees. "It's just us. You have to help me stand up. Do you hear me, Pa? You have to stand before Burke comes back again. We have to get you back to the clinic. No one else is going to help us. We'll have to do it ourselves."

No, that's not true, he thought as he struggled to lift his father. *That's what Grandpa would have said, but it's not true.*

Patrick grunted with the effort of trying to hoist his father to his feet. As thin as he was, his father was still too heavy—or Patrick was too weak. As he prayed for help, they tumbled once more, and Patrick panted in exhaustion. His eyes darted to the dark shadows, sure that Burke was just waiting for the others to leave before he returned.

"I'm sorry, Pa," he whispered. "I can't do it all alone. I never could. I need help."

He listened to the sounds of the rain, the river, the men shouting in the distance.

What happened to Grandpa and the others? he wondered. *And Burke?*

As if in answer, he heard one set of uncertain footsteps. The footsteps came closer. *If that's Burke, he'll run right into us.*

Patrick looked around for a place to hide. The riverbank just above him was too steep to drag his father up by himself. He could see no trees close enough to hide behind, no bushes, only the river to his left. It *was* dark, but someone with a lantern would have no problem seeing them.

All right, Pa, let's go.

Quietly he dragged his father into the water once more, and the current seemed to pull at him, tugging him downstream. Trying not to shiver, he crouched in the shallows to hide, making sure his father's face was above water. He heard the footsteps once more, closer, then close enough to touch. Someone breathing hard, as if he had been running. And he still couldn't tell who it was.

"Patrick!" someone yelled from a distance. The footsteps paused and the breathing stopped, as if the person was listening. Patrick thought he could hear his grandfather calling, far away, and then it was silent once again.

"Patrick! Where are . . ." came the voice again, even farther away.

Still the dark figure paused, and Patrick didn't dare look, didn't dare to show his face for fear it would shine in the dimmest light.

Patrick felt the mud beneath his feet shift, then he slid with his father backward into a deeper pool in the river. In a moment it was over his head, and he was sputtering and gasping for breath, trying to hold his father up.

He tried not to splash but he couldn't help it. A moment later the dark figure pounced on him and grabbed Patrick's arms with strong hands.

"No, let me go!" yelled Patrick. "Grandpa! Ma!" he shouted at the top of his lungs, thrashing and kicking as hard as he could. "Over here!"

The person who had grabbed him didn't run, only held Patrick even more tightly with one arm while he collected Patrick's father out of the river with his other. He dragged them both into shallower water.

"Hold still, Patrick," said the dark figure. "I'm not who you think I am."

Patrick stopped when he realized the voice did not belong to Conrad Burke.

"It's you," Patrick whispered, glad to let Dr. Thompson help him and his father to safety.

Mr. McWaid was shivering, still breathing and mumbling something Patrick couldn't make out.

"I don't know why you were hiding, Patrick," said the doctor, "but let's get you both back to the clinic."

"Patrick!" someone yelled from just a few yards away this time. "Are you down there?"

A moment later they were surrounded by Patrick's family. The Old Man was there, along with Mrs. McWaid, Becky, and Michael.

"I found Pa," gasped Patrick. "I mean, *we* found him."

Mrs. McWaid dropped to her knees, wrapped her arms around her husband, and cried as the Old Man propped them both up. Patrick wasn't sure if his father was quite aware of everything going on, but at least he was alive. Becky wrapped a blanket around them from the wagon, and Michael jumped up and down, trying to hug his father, too.

"Is he all right?" asked Michael over and over. "Did we really find him? I knew it, Patrick! I knew we would find him. Didn't I tell you we would find him? I just *knew*—"

"Sure, and we'll have plenty of time for this later, Michael," interrupted their grandfather. Patrick heard the urgent tone of his voice. "But the doctor's right. We need to get him back to the clinic right away."

"John, can you hear me?" asked their mother, looking into her husband's face. "You're free."

Mr. McWaid nodded weakly but couldn't say anything. He raised his hand to hold hers, and it was shaking.

"Here, boys, help me get him up the riverbank," commanded the Old Man.

Patrick glanced up to see where they were going. Above them he could see the outline of a hunched-over man, standing between them and where they had to go. Lanterns flickered from somewhere behind him.

Conrad Burke. Again!

CHAPTER 25

CONFESSION

For a moment Patrick didn't say anything; he just put all his strength into helping to lift his father up and away from the river. With the Old Man on one side and the doctor and Patrick on the other, they formed a kind of chair for Mr. McWaid and walked him up the slope.

"That's far enough," growled Burke as they walked up to him with their load. "Put him down there."

Patrick thought he saw a gun in the man's hand, but Burke didn't bother to point it at them.

"Grandpa!" Becky yelled in warning, but like Patrick, their grandfather had already seen the man.

"It's over, Mr. Burke," ordered the Old Man. "You don't have a prayer of getting away from this place."

"I don't need to get away anymore. I was going to make it look like an accident. Now I just need to complete my job."

Burke coughed, his lungs rattling. The way he gripped his side told Patrick that he was badly injured.

"It's too late for that, Burke," the Old Man went on. "Your friend back home in Ireland confessed. The police know all about you now."

"I don't believe you." Burke almost laughed. "Now, put him down or—"

"I think he's been shot, Grandfather," whispered Patrick. "During the chase after the tiger."

Patrick quietly slipped away from his father and stepped up to the man who had followed them halfway around the world. The man who had meant to kill his pa.

"Patrick, no!" cried Mrs. McWaid, but she needn't have worried. Conrad Burke gasped and crumpled to the ground as a group of men with lanterns came up behind him. A small curved stick—not a gun—fell from his hand.

Somehow it didn't seem right to Patrick to go back to school just two days later, back to ciphering and geography and grammar. Pa was in the clinic, but he was already doing better, sitting up in bed, even telling a few jokes. Patrick's mother wouldn't let go of his hand.

Their mother had also insisted that Patrick, Becky, and Michael return to class. And there *was* one highlight, after all, one that they didn't want to miss: Prince Alfred's visit to their school.

"Class, His Majesty Prince Alfred is about to return to England." Miss Tyler was beaming in her finest dress. She had already curtsied three times and nearly fainted twice. Every student in the room was sitting arrow-straight with hands folded in front. "But before he does, he's asked to say a few words to us."

Everyone applauded politely, and a few glanced at Patrick, but Patrick just grinned. He had no idea what the prince was going to say.

Standing at the head of the class in a freshly starched blue military uniform, Prince Alfred cleared his throat.

"Thank you, ah, Miss Tyler. You're very kind to allow me this opportunity to visit. It's been a remarkable week. I've stayed in Echuca several days longer than I'd expected. Truly, it was only meant to be a quick visit, but . . ."

The smile never left Miss Tyler's face as he continued, describing some of their adventures and the things that had happened to them in the past several days.

"I would also like to take this opportunity to thank two of the bravest and most clever young people I've ever had the pleasure to meet—Rebecca and Patrick McWaid."

This time the class all looked at Patrick and Becky, even Sebastian. Patrick slid down a little lower in his chair.

"It was Rebecca's—oh, forgive me, she prefers 'Becky'—it was Becky's idea to fashion a rescue device with a cannon that saved the lives of an entire boatload of people, including myself. Incredibly clever. Please stand up, Rebecca."

Crimson-faced, Becky stood at her table while the others clapped. Patrick heard the door quietly open, and he turned around to see his grandfather standing in the back of the classroom, hugging the wall. The prince nodded at him as he continued.

"And it was her brother Patrick whose concern for his father led to the arrest of a very dangerous criminal. He's a determined boy, is he not, Captain?"

Patrick's grandfather looked to the side quickly, as if there might be some other "captain."

"Aye, he is that, Your Majesty. My grandson is a fighter . . . in his own way. As sure as you're born, he is."

Patrick's grandfather winked at him as the prince cleared his throat.

"It's thanks to Patrick—and his sister—that I can offer complete absolution for their father, John McWaid."

A small hand rose in the first row. Startled, Prince Alfred smiled down at the little girl while Miss Tyler tried without success to wave her down.

"What's absolution?" piped up Edwina before anyone could stop her.

The prince chuckled. "I beg your pardon, I shouldn't use such big words. Absolution is a sort of forgiveness. It's as if he never committed any crimes, which in this case, he actually never did."

Now they believe me and Becky, thought Patrick. *They finally believe us!*

"It's a marvelous story, really," the prince went on. "Especially now that the *real* criminal is recovering from his injuries in the safety of a Melbourne prison."

"The bad man went to jail?" asked Edwina.

"That's right. He was accidentally shot in all the confusion the other night. And once they captured him, an imprisoned outlaw named Hookey Simpson told the police much more about this Burke fellow."

"What did he say?" asked Patrick.

"It seems the two had been working together to try to capture Patrick and Rebecca's—ah, that is, Patrick and Becky's father."

Patrick closed his eyes for a second, hanging on to every word. Even his bandaged head didn't hurt as much where he had been hit by the tiger-hunter's club.

"The tigers." Edwina held up her hand once more. "Did you ever see the tigers? My brother saw them. One ran right past our house."

"I understand a tiger was captured here in your town the day after the circus barges' accident on the river," replied the prince, looking at Miss Tyler, who nodded. "Another was netted after it swam across to the other side of the river, and the third shot in the leg by a farmer up the river a way. That *is* the one we saw, was it not, Patrick?"

Patrick nodded and the prince continued.

"All three are going to be fine, and they've already been put on a barge down the river. Which means 'Michael McWaid and His Wild Animal Show' will now be the finest act in Echuca."

The whole class laughed. Even Jack Duggan had taken time away from his job at the boatyard to come to school that morning. Miss Tyler had looked at him curiously as he took an open seat in the front row of tables.

"Splendid, Michael," said the prince. "Do show them your bear, the way you showed me. That is, if it's all right with Miss Tyler."

Michael shyly joined Prince Alfred at the front of the class, pulling his pet koala, Christopher, carefully out of a crate. The little animal climbed to his shoulders and stayed there.

Patrick put a hand to his head as he laughed. It still hurt, but he didn't care. *I'll be fine—as long as I don't have to do any more tightrope acts. Not even Michael could get me to say yes!*

THE REAL 1868

Many of the events in this story are based on true-life accounts of the years just before and after 1868. Remember the tightrope walker? That really happened in Echuca during that time, although the person who performed many of the tightrope shows (a young man named Tommy Freeman) carried people across the river on his back, not in a wheelbarrow. The actual wheelbarrow act belonged to a French performer named Blondin, who lived and performed at that time in Europe and North America.

The circus also traveled in those days, and there is a historic account of a barge sinking in a river close to the Murray. Several elephants had to swim ashore. Besides that, barges on the Murray were often leaky and sank.

And speaking of sinking, logs coming down the Murray River presented a serious hazard to paddle steamers. That's what inspired the part of the story when the *Lady Elisabeth* sank at Boomerang Bend.

The harpoon cannon, which Becky used to rescue the people on the sinking *Lady Elisabeth*, had been invented a few years before, in the early 1800s. They were also used by rescue teams to shoot ropes with anchors to help save people and ships.

Perhaps most important to our story, Prince Alfred, duke of Edinburgh, was a real man. And he did visit Australia in 1868—the first royal visit to the colony. He did not make it to Echuca or ride on a Murray River paddle steamer, but that's where the "fiction" part of "historical fiction" comes in. Blending fact with the imaginary, what actually happened with what might have been. In 1868 there was always a lot of excitement in frontier Australia, and plenty more in store for Patrick, Becky, and Michael.

Be sure to read Book 4 in the exciting
ADVENTURES DOWN UNDER!
Dingo Creek Challenge

When Patrick and his sister, Becky, are caught in the middle of a scuffle between settlers and aborigines, a challenge game of cricket seems like a great way to bring the two sides together. But when the aborigines are accused of stealing settlers' horses, it's up to Patrick and Becky to uncover the truth—before the friendly match turns into an all-out battle!

Series for Middle Graders*
From Bethany House Publishers

ADVENTURES DOWN UNDER · by Robert Elmer
When Patrick McWaid's father is unjustly sent to Australia as a prisoner in 1867, the rest of the family follows, uncovering action-packed mystery along the way.

ADVENTURES OF THE NORTHWOODS · by Lois Walfrid Johnson
Kate O'Connell and her stepbrother Anders encounter mystery and adventure in northwest Wisconsin near the turn of the century.

AN AMERICAN ADVENTURE SERIES · by Lee Roddy
Hildy Corrigan and her family must overcome danger and hardship during the Great Depression as they search for a "forever home."

BLOODHOUNDS, INC. · by Bill Myers
Hilarious, hair-raising suspense follows brother-and-sister detectives Sean and Melissa Hunter in these madcap mysteries with a message.

JOURNEYS TO FAYRAH · by Bill Myers
Join Denise, Nathan, and Josh on amazing journeys as they discover the wonders and lessons of the mystical Kingdom of Fayrah.

MANDIE BOOKS · by Lois Gladys Leppard
With over four million sold, the turn-of-the-century adventures of Mandie and her many friends will keep readers eager for more.

THE RIVERBOAT ADVENTURES · by Lois Walfrid Johnson
Libby Norstad and her friend Caleb face the challenges and risks of working with the Underground Railroad during the mid–1800s.

TRAILBLAZER BOOKS · by Dave and Neta Jackson
Follow the exciting lives of real-life Christian heroes through the eyes of child characters as they share their faith and God's love with others around the world.

THE TWELVE CANDLES CLUB · by Elaine L. Schulte
When four twelve-year-old girls set up a business doing odd jobs and baby-sitting, they find themselves in the midst of wacky adventures and hilarious surprises.

THE YOUNG UNDERGROUND · by Robert Elmer
Peter and Elise Andersen's plots to protect their friends and themselves from Nazi soldiers in World War II Denmark guarantee fast-paced action and suspenseful reads.

*(ages 8–13)